ASSUMPTION

ANNE SIMS

Assumption
Copyright © 2024 by Anne Sims

All rights reserved. No part of this publication
may be reproduced, distributed, or transmitted
in any form or by any means, including
photocopying, recording, or other electronic
or mechanical methods, without the prior
written permission of the author, except
in the case of brief quotations embodied
in critical reviews and certain other non-
commercial uses permitted by copyright law.

Tellwell Talent
www.tellwell.ca

ISBN
978-0-2288-7416-4 (Hardcover)
978-0-2288-7415-7 (Paperback)
978-0-2288-7417-1 (eBook)

For my children,
Those were the years...

PREFACE

At the time this novel occurs, the terms "First Nations" and "Indigenous" were not in use. To keep the story true to its time I refer to First Nations peoples using the colloquial terms in common use at the time.

CHAPTER 1

In the silence broken by the squawking of mating crows and raucous calls of seagulls, I hear a truck bouncing down the rutted road followed by the clang of the mailbox's door. It is a welcome interruption to my day, which I am spending sorting out her possessions—not that there were that many. The kitchen cupboards are filled with dented pots and pans and chipped dishes I remember from our years at the lighthouse. In the sitting room the shelves on each side of the fireplace are crammed with books, magazines and records. For most of our childhoods, Matt's and my knowledge of the world outside our rocky windswept island was informed by a dog-eared set of the Encyclopedia Britannica and stacks of National Geographic magazines dating back twenty years or more. Once a month, weather permitting, the supply ship carrying our groceries and items from the Eaton's catalogue would also deliver the latest edition of National Geographic and a treasure trove of books selected by Mother and Uncle Alex. On many a winter evening, when wild storms battered and screeched against the windows, doors and walls, we devoured articles about exotic animals and places and adventurous explorers who roamed through worlds alien to our own surroundings. On those housebound nights, Uncle Alex would read or tell us tales about sea monsters and the heroic feats of pirates and other seafarers. If our attention flagged or we became fidgety, he would wiggle his finger at us and, in his foghorn voice, say, "Now pay attention, wee bairns, ye never know when ye may be called upon to rescue yourself or someone else."

Tripping over stacks of half-packed boxes, I grab Uncle's old yellow mac off its hook and run down the road, hoping to catch the mailman before he drives away. Mother's house is at the end of a track that runs into a rock-strewn beach. I wouldn't be surprised to know that the mail truck was the only vehicle to travel down this forlorn, overgrown road, which is at least half a mile from the nearest neighbour. Running down the road, I call out, "Hi, I'm Laura MacLeod, Elizabeth's daughter!"

"Pleased to meet you. I'm Phil Bailey. I'm sorry about your loss."

"Did you know my mother?"

"Nope, can't say I did. I've been driving this route the last seven years, but I can count on the fingers of one hand the times I saw her outside the house. Occasionally I'd see her in town, but she was always alone and avoided eye contact."

"Do you know if she had any contact with neighbours?"

"Well, old Mrs. McKinley, whose house you passed on the way here, said that she knew your Uncle Alex, a lighthouse keeper who would come on his time off, and who settled here after he retired. She said he would visit her once in a while, but never with your mother, who he said was not much for socializing. He died before I started the route, so I never met him. Did you know him?"

"Yeah, my brother and I grew up at the lighthouse. Our father was killed in the war, and we went to live with my mother's brother Uncle Alex when I was three or four. Mother was expecting Matt."

"Are you going to be around for a while?"

"No, I've been here almost a week and have to get back to my teaching job in Whitehorse."

"So I guess there won't be a service."

"No, Mother wasn't religious, and the only family she had was Matt and me. Matt lives in Nova Scotia, and in the summer he and I will return and take her ashes to the lighthouse, where we will scatter them in the sea."

"Well then, I suppose I won't be seeing you again. Oh, I almost forgot. There's some junk mail and a letter for your mom. Same one as usual, with the black cross on the back of the envelope. Have a safe journey home."

Walking back to the house, I stuff the mail in my pocket and think about the word "home." Since I left the lighthouse, I haven't considered many of the places that I have lived in as home. Robert Frost said that home is the place that when you return, they must take you in. Well, in the twenty years since I left the lighthouse, there hasn't been a "they" to take me in. Not that I ever needed a they.

A thick fog rolls in as I trudge back toward the house, muffling the sound of Phil's truck and obscuring the offshore reefs. The silence is as dense as the fog and the shadowy outlines of the moss-draped firs and cedars appear like sentinels guarding Mother's ramshackle house from intruders. Going back into the darkened kitchen, I light the lamps and stoke the fire, all the while wondering how she could have spent the last five years here by herself without going mad.

Since Uncle Alex died five years ago, I have only been back once to see Mother. Without his robust presence and hearty laugh, the house is cheerless and depressing. Mother seemed to withdraw into a world of her own, and after a few years she shut off the phone service. Although Matt and I wrote her the occasional letters, we never received replies. We assumed she wanted to be left alone, but seeing the diminished conditions in which she was living, I wonder if she couldn't afford the phone service. A week ago, I got a scribbled note from her saying that she was ill and needed me. I can never remember her ever saying that she needed me. It had always been Uncle Alex and sometimes Matt that she called upon.

It had taken me three days to arrange for a substitute teacher, get a flight to "outside," rent a car, and take a ferry to Nanaimo on British Columbia's Vancouver Island. From there, through the howling wind and lashing rain, I drove the winding roads across the island to the west coast. Arriving in darkness, the house seemed deserted. The windows were dark and there was no smoke from the chimney. In my headlights, I saw Uncle Alex's broken-down car resting in knee-high grass and weeds. As I entered the unlocked door, the stench of untended illness made me recoil. "Mother?" I called, but the only response was a soft moaning from her bedroom. My heart weeps as I recall the moment I saw her huddled in a fetal position and wrapped in a ragged quilt. I hardly recognized the skeletal figure with shrunken cheeks and disheveled grey hair. The last time I saw Mother she looked middle-aged, but now she looked twenty or thirty years older. Her eyelids fluttered when I touched her ice-cold hands and said, "I'm here, Mother," but other than that she showed no response. I knew she desperately needed to get to the hospital, but at that late hour and hearing the growing intensity of the storm, I knew it would be safer to wait until dawn.

I wrapped Mother in the few moth-hole-riddled blankets that I could find, laid her on the couch near the fireplace and sat by her comatose body until first light. By then the brunt of the storm had passed. I made a bed for her on the back seat of the car, on which I laid her frail body, which couldn't have weighed more than ninety pounds. For the first thirty miles the road was horrendous. Every time I hit a pothole or drove over tree branches, a moan rose from behind me. Not knowing if I was talking to her or myself, I kept saying, "We'll be there soon. I'm so sorry, Mother, the doctors will help you. Please don't die, I need you." At times my tears flowed as heavy as the rain on the windshield.

As it turned out, her body was riddled with cancer. Looking at me accusingly, the doctor said, "Why did you wait so long to get her help? She must have been in pain for months." I sat with her for three days listening to her calling out, "Michael, Michael, where are you?" I knew Michael wasn't her husband's or father's name, so why Michael? But then, Mother's life had always been somewhat of a mystery to me.

Finally, as the first light streamed through the window and lit up her white-draped body, her eyes opened wide and she gave a deep sigh. Then she was gone. I sat by her shrunken body for a few hours, remembering our years together. Although I never really knew or understood her, or understood the bond between her and Matthew, I loved her and mourned what could have been.

It is noon in Halifax, so I call Matt at work.

"She's gone, Matt."

"What, so soon? Do you want me to come out?"

"Not now. Come in the summer and we'll take her ashes to the lighthouse. Is there anything in the house that you would like?"

"Well, I'll think about it. Uncle Alex kept a lighthouse log and I think Mother wrote in a journal. Do you think they are still in the house?"

"I'll look and let you know."

"Thanks for being there, Laura. I'm glad Mother didn't die alone. You were always better than me at looking after things."

Assumption

By the time I finish arrangements at the funeral home in town and drive back to Mother's house, the roads have been cleared of the storm's offerings and the potholes graded. The windswept sky is a brilliant, cloudless blue, and the trees and bushes look like they have been freshly laundered and hung out to dry. Tiny sparkling droplets hang precariously from the needled branches, the budding leaves of the alder trees look like millions of verdant polka dots silhouetted against a painted backdrop, and the big-leaf maples sport clumps of pollen-filled sacs. Opening all the car windows, I greedily inhale the day-soft scent of early spring.

On dark, stormy days at the lighthouse, Mother would retreat to her room, shut the door and play dirge-like classical music on her ancient record player. On one such day, Uncle Alex was away and Matt slipped and fell on some seaweed-covered rocks. I ran up to the house and burst into Mother's room, yelling, "Matt's fallen on the rocks and cut himself badly!" Mother sprang up from her bed, knocked over the Victrola and rushed out the door, but not before I noticed the tears running down her cheeks. One day shortly before I left for university, Uncle Alex surprised Mother with a piano, which he had transported by barge to the lighthouse from an old Anglican church up the coast that had shut its doors. Much to Matt's and my surprise, Mother turned out to be an excellent pianist, and even though she didn't have any books or sheet music, she had an amazing repertoire of classical and popular music. That old piano still sits in the living room, but if its covering of dust says anything, it hasn't been opened or played for years.

On days like today she would open all the doors and windows and cook and clean with frantic energy. Work done, she would throw her apron over a chair and pack a picnic lunch, and we would set off to spend the afternoon exploring the shores of our rock-bound home. Matt and I would play in the warm tide pools and search for clams, oysters and sea asparagus while Mother would seek out wildflowers, stopping often to breathe in the salty sea-scented air. However, if a boat approached she would hastily retreat to the house where visitors were never invited. Uncle Alex would handle all the business and deliveries at the dock, and if by chance some stranded mariners ended up on our island, they were accommodated in a small cottage which at one time had housed an assistant lighthouse keeper.

The fire has gone out at the house, and it feels cold and smells musty. Looking at what needs to be sorted out and packed, I think that if I hurry I can be away by morning. Before I had left town I'd met with a real estate agent to handle the sale of the house and told him, "I won't be taking much with me, so if you know of people who would want some of the stuff, give it to them and the rest can go to the dump."

On the couch I pile up the things that Matt and I want to keep: a photo of Uncle Alex in his yellow mac and rain hat standing in front of the lighthouse, a photo of Matt, the lighthouse logs, Uncle Alex's barometer and Bible, Mother's pearl necklace and earrings that she would wear for Christmas dinner, a gold wedding band she said she never wore because it was too small, and a beautiful perfume bottle that was empty but still carried traces of an exotic scent. Finally, I take the picture albums from the fireplace shelves and quickly leaf through them. I had never noticed before that, though there are pictures of the lighthouse, Uncle Alex, Matt and me, there aren't any pictures of Mother or of anything that preceded our arrival at the lighthouse. I check everywhere but can't find Mother's journal.

Looking around for something to pack everything in, I remember an old suitcase stored in the cupboard under the staircase where we never ventured because Uncle Alex would say, "Beware of the sea mooglies who live there." After all these years the suitcase is musty and mildewed, but it's large enough to hold all the items on the couch. I line the bottom with the yellow mac, fill it and squeeze it shut. After searching in drawers and cupboards, I finally find the suitcase keys as well as Mother's purse, filled with unpaid bills.

I tumble out of bed before sunrise, as I have a long day ahead of me. By the time I haul my suitcases out to the car and lock the house, the sky is lightening up. These few minutes between the night and the dawn have always been my favourite time. The emerging light casts moving, glimmering shadows on the water and the trees stand still, holding their breath in anticipation of a new day. For a few brief moments the world is silent as if on the verge of a new creation. As I drive away toward the rising sun, I resist the temptation to look back.

CHAPTER 2

Even the brilliant sky and hosts of bright yellow daffodils surrounding the airport parking lot do little to raise my spirits. The flowers bring back too many memories. Come February, whether it was sleeting, blowing or raining, Mother would put on Uncle's mac and head outdoors, searching for the first sighting of green fingers poking through the sodden soil. In every pocket of dirt on our barren, rocky island, she planted crocuses, hyacinths, daffodils, tulips and other bulbs whose names I can't remember. She was always gathering seaweed, leaves, other bits of greenery and kitchen scraps to add to her precious compost pile.

My flight is running late. Usually I'm impatient with delay, but today I'm feeling exhausted and in no hurry to return to my classroom of hormone-fuelled teenagers. Tomorrow will be a demanding day. From past experiences I've found that most substitute teachers don't deal well with adolescents who delight in pushing their buttons. It usually takes me a few days to restore some semblance of order. Right now I'm not sure if I will have the patience or energy to play the enforcer.

Looking back, I'm not sure why I chose to be a teacher. Late one night, I came downstairs for a drink of water and heard Uncle Alex and Mother arguing.

"She's too young, Alex. I don't want her to leave. She's safe here."

"Elizabeth, you can't protect her forever. Laura has been here for most of her life and now it is time for you to let go and find her own way. And in four years it will be time for Matthew to go also."

"But I'm so fearful for them, and for me."

"They will be okay. They are smart, independent kids and it is time for them to discover a world and a life beyond the lighthouse and our isolated lives. I will surely miss them too."

"Oh, you're probably right, but I'll find it hard not to worry."

"Elizabeth, fourteen years ago you chose how and where to live your life, and now they should have the same opportunity."

Up until then, Matt and I had done our schooling through correspondence. As soon as breakfast was over we would sit at the kitchen table until lunch and work on the current set of lessons, which the supply boat would deliver once a month. I loved learning and usually scored an A in my assignments. Often, Uncle Alex and Mother's book order arrived at the same time, but we weren't allowed to delve into them until after we had done our chores and finished lunch. Later, at university, I realized that I was already familiar with most of the books on the reading lists for my English and history courses.

After lunch I would curl up in a chair beside the fireplace or, weather permitting, find a sunny, sheltered spot on the rocks and lose myself in whatever book I was reading. On the other hand, Matt would bolt out of the door and not return until dinner or dusk. The shelves and cupboards in his room spilled over with all his finds: shells, dried crabs, nets, stones, skeletal remains of sea life, driftwood, bird feathers and the coloured glass bulbs used by Japanese fishermen to float and mark their nets. One time he found an intact coconut, which he cracked open and gave us a taste of a fruit that Uncle Alex said had probably drifted thousands of miles from its tropical home.

As Matt grew older, Uncle Alex would get him to help in the lighthouse. By the time he was twelve, Matt knew how to operate most of the instruments and the light and was often better than the barometer at predicting changes in the weather and the onset of winter storms. Sometimes during storms, boats would founder on the offshore reefs and rocks and Uncle Alex and Matt would row out and rescue the stranded crews. Mother would be frantic with worry, but Uncle Alex would try to calm her fears by saying, "Don't worry, lass, we know what we're doing, and all will be safe and well." I think that if anything had ever happened to Matt, Mother would have gone mad. Although she never said as much, I assumed that Matt was her favourite child. Whenever I tried to help her in the kitchen, she would say, "Oh, never mind, Laura. It's easier to do it myself." Yet she never refused Matt's help.

Looking at us, you would never know that we were mother and daughter. Like Matt, she had fair hair and skin and was slight and small boned, whereas I had dark hair and olive skin and was sturdy. She was affectionate with Matt, but if I tried to hug her she would stiffen up and draw back. It was Uncle Alex to whom I went when I needed comforting or affection.

Shortly after that late-night discussion about my future, university calendars and applications began to arrive on the supply boat. Although I had mixed feelings about leaving home, I was excited by the prospect of exploring new ideas, relationships and environments. My ideas about the outside world were coloured by books and magazines and our summer holidays near the fishing community close to our summer cottage. I pored over the calendars, absorbing information about all the interesting courses that I could take, and thought about the friends and maybe even a boyfriend I might meet. Looking back, I realize now that I was naive and overly optimistic.

Other than one dress I would wear for Christmas or Easter dinner and the rare summer trip into town, my wardrobe consisted of dungarees, T-shirts, warm sweaters, jackets, a yellow mac and rain hat, running shoes and boots. Perusing Eaton's winter and spring catalogues, Mother and I spent hours deciding on a going-to-school wardrobe. Mother knew that Uncle Alex's salary would be stretched to pay for my tuition and board, so we didn't consider any frills or luxuries. Still, we were excited when our order arrived and our purchases spilled out of the string-tied brown-paper parcels: sturdy brown Oxfords, a grey worsted skirt and jacket, two white blouses, two warm sweaters, a pair of plaid wool pants, sturdy underwear and socks, a trench coat and two pairs of flannel pyjamas, all costing the exorbitant sum of three hundred dollars. After trying everything on and stripping off the tags, we packed most of it into a new suitcase. Matt's comment was, "With all those big-city clothes, you would think that you were going to be a socialite instead of a university student. When I go away to school, my present clothes will just do me fine," which I think was his way of saying, "I'm going to miss you."

It was only when we were doing the final preparations that it really hit all of us that I was actually going to leave. Other than spending my first four years elsewhere, my last fourteen years had been mostly spent within the familiar confines of my family and our little isolated rock-strewn island. When I questioned Mother about that "elsewhere," or about my father, she would become tight-lipped and say, "Your father died in the war, and it was so long ago I don't remember much." And that was that.

On the provincial exams I made top grades, so I knew my application to the University of British Columbia would be accepted. I would have liked to have gone farther afield, but Uncle Alex had an old friend in Vancouver, Mrs. Esplen, with whom I could board. I chose the education faculty because, if Uncle

Alex's funds ran out, after two years I could start to teach and finish my degree in summer school. Also, between Christmas and Easter breaks and long summer holidays I assumed that I could return often to my beloved lighthouse home. Now, twenty years later, I wonder if I would have chosen differently if I could have seen the future.

As September drew closer, everyone seemed tense and distracted. I ran around the island visiting my favourite spots, and packed and repacked my suitcase. Matt hung around, bringing me some of his beachcombing treasures, "So you won't miss or forget us." Uncle Alex kept telling me stories from his UBC days, "So it won't seem so strange to you, lass." Mother became increasingly frantic, trying to cram into a few weeks a survival guide for living in the outside world. "Study hard and do well, Laura. This is a wonderful opportunity for you, one that I wish had been there for me."

A book explaining the facts of life was left on my bed. "Forget about the boys, Laura, they'll only distract you from your studies and get you into trouble. People are nosy, but remember your affairs are nobody's business but your own. Stay away from alcohol, as it can destroy your life, and pick your friends carefully. There are a lot of snakes out there who, if you're not careful, will destroy you." In the few weeks before my departure, Mother gave me more advice and showed more concern than she had in my previous eighteen years. Looking back now, I realize how naive and trusting I was and how scared she was for me. I should have paid more attention to her advice, but what did I know of the world beyond our isolated island.

I awoke early to an eerie calm. For the previous week the lighthouse's foghorn had bleated continuously, and the ocean and reefs were obscured by a dense, unrelenting fog. But on that day, as if I were receiving a going-away gift, the sun rose over the horizon, wrapping the water with shimmering foils of orange and scarlet. Not a sound, not even the calls of early rising gulls or trees shaking off their night slumbers, could be heard. In the silence I began to have misgivings and fears about the journey and adventure that I would embark on in a few hours. How could I leave the only home I had ever known? How could I leave the people I loved and who loved me? What if I failed? With an uneasy heart, I realized that it was too late to turn back to the secure world of my childhood.

As the sunrise faded, I heard the clang of kitchen pots and Uncle Alex calling up the stairs, "Get up, wee bairns. It's time to get started on the day." I poured cold water in the bowl, splashed it on my face, braided my hair and put on my new sweater, pants and shoes. They felt stiff and confining, and I glanced longingly at my worn jeans and shirts hanging on the wall pegs. Mother had prepared a holiday breakfast, but she was so anxious and distracted that she burnt the scones and overcooked the eggs and sausages. Too soon we heard the familiar rumble of the supply boat. Matt hauled my suitcase down to the dock with Mother following, carrying enough lunch to last us a week. Uncle Alex was accompanying me to Vancouver to help me get settled. As well as it being against the regulations, he was uneasy about leaving Matt in charge of the lighthouse, but Mother adamantly refused to let another keeper on our island while Uncle Alex was away. Matt pressed his favourite stone in my hand and Mother hugged me as if she would never see me again. As the supply boat pulled away from the dock, I could see tears running down her cheeks and Matt biting his lip, trying not to cry. I kept looking back at them until they disappeared. With a heavy heart and churning stomach, I turned and looked ahead.

CHAPTER 3

During the choppy voyage to Nanaimo I was more homesick than seasick, and Uncle Alex became the dour Scot he always claimed to be. We saw several breaching whales who, like me, were probably setting off for their southbound winter journey. Other than spending three weeks every summer at Uncle Alex's west coast summer cottage five miles from Tofino, this was my first time so far away from the lighthouse. Our first three days at the cottage were spent getting rid of the mice, airing out the house and bedding, cutting back the encroaching growth and getting the old car running again. Then we would change into our good clothes and drive into town for supplies.

Mother would give Uncle Alex her list, but she would never come with us. Shopping done, Uncle Alex would head to the tavern, setting us free to explore. In our haste to be off, we scarcely heard his instructions: "Don't talk to strangers, watch out for cars and be back here by five o'clock." To Matt and me, the small town was a big city. Unused to traffic, we didn't dare cross the streets until there wasn't a car in sight. We argued over how to spend our five dollars of birthday money: candy or a book; a hamburger and fries with pop; a box of chocolates for Mother; a game; or, if it was Saturday, we might go to the community hall to watch a cowboy film. My favourite movies featured Roy Rogers and Dale Evans, but Matt preferred the Lone Ranger. After our money was spent we would head to the docks, where the fishermen would be unloading large catches of salmon and halibut or repairing their nets and equipment. Teasingly, they would call out, "Hey, young fella, wanna help us gut some fish? Hey, pretty girl, we need a cook on our boat." I was too shy to banter with these dark-skinned strangers, but Matt would chat with them and sometimes we would be invited onto their boats for a cup of cocoa. Before he was hired as a lighthouse keeper, Uncle Alex spent about ten years trawling on his boat, *Rover*. Two or three times a week Uncle Alex would visit with his old friends in town, but after the novelty of the big city wore off we preferred to explore the waters and forests around our cottage. Mother never seemed to worry when we took off in our old rowboat for an afternoon, or spent the day in the woods. Occasionally she would pack a lunch and join us, and she was always in high spirits. We never saw anyone, so I guess she figured we were safe.

After a three-hour bus ride to Nanaimo, we boarded the Canadian Pacific Railway ferry to Vancouver. My stomach had recovered and I ate a hearty supper in the elegant dining room. White linen tablecloths and napkins, silver utensils and teapots, Chinese waiters in long white aprons and a large selection of choices were an exotic contrast to our oilcloth table covering, cracked dishes, plain food and Mother in her patched, worn apron back home.

Arriving in Vancouver in the dark and a torrential downpour, I was completely disoriented by the masses of people, tall buildings, lights and noise. By the time we arrived at Mrs. Esplen's home I was half asleep, but aware that my usual nighttime lullaby of wind, surf and rain would probably be replaced by the beeping of horns, the wailing of sirens and the screeching of tires.

It was odd to note Uncle Alex's behaviour with my new landlady. Although I had only experienced kindness and concern from him, he was, like many Scots, not overly effusive or affectionate. However, when Mrs. Esplen opened the door he scooped her up, kissing and hugging her. With tears running down her cheeks, she said, "Alex, you big oaf, put me down and introduce me. This pretty girl must be Laura." Soon after, "Norah Dear"—as Uncle Alex called her—tucked me under a fluffy quilt and I quickly fell asleep. A few times during the night I woke and heard their muted voices and laughter. Strange, I thought, that Uncle Alex had never mentioned Norah Dear before. I had always assumed that Mother, Matt and I were his only loves.

For the next few days Uncle Alex shepherded me around Vancouver. Our first stop was the Bank of Montreal, where he opened an account in my name and deposited $300. "Your room and board and tuition have been paid, and if you are thrifty the money should see you through until you come home for Christmas." Wow! $300. The most money I'd had up to then was a five-dollar birthday gift. I felt like I had won the Irish sweepstakes, which Uncle Alex bought a ticket for every year. "When I win I'll take us all back to Scotland. We are Highland Scots, descendants of Robert the Bruce. I was born in Edinburgh, but before my parents emigrated to Canada when I was fifteen, we traversed the country from east to west and north to south. After all these decades, the heather-clad hills and the shining lochs still call to me. In truth, I have never entirely left my first home, and my desire is to be buried there among my MacLeod ancestors."

Our next stop was the university, where I bought the required texts and supplies at the bookstore. I still have my 1943-published copy of *The College Survey of English Literature*. Even though it was almost new, we were able to find it for half price: five dollars. After twenty years it is dog-eared, underlined and annotated. I think of it as my personal Bible.

The campus was noisy and confusing, and navigating from building to building seemed a daunting task. Until then, Matt and I had used the stars, the sun and our compasses to find our way. Now all I had was a map with confusing symbols and a legend. "Don't worry, lassie, soon it will become very familiar." Even the professors' and students' attire was strange. Uncle Alex had one black going-to-funerals suit, whereas the professors dashing around the campus wore variously coloured suits and sports jackets. I soon realized that the Eaton's wardrobe that Mother and I had picked out bore little resemblance to the clothes that most of the girls were wearing. With my long braided hair and sturdy Oxfords, I was already beginning to feel like a misfit. The braids would have to go, but how did the girls get their hair to look so full and high? Where did they get their black and white shoes that I later learned were called saddle shoes?

On the night before he left, Uncle Alex took Norah Dear and me to the White Spot for dinner. What a feast! I still remember the aroma of fluffy buttermilk biscuits with greengage jam, heaping baskets of golden-fried chicken in the straw, thick chocolate milkshakes and boysenberry pie topped with soft ice cream. Even the gourmet dinners that in later years I enjoyed in fancy Parisian cafés never matched my recollection of my first restaurant meal in Vancouver.

Before I went to bed that night, Uncle Alex said, "Work hard, Laura, so we'll be proud of your success. We'll be counting the weeks until you come home at Christmas. If you have any problems, talk to Norah. She's a loving woman and knows that the world out there can at times be scary and hurtful." Weeping silently, I lay awake in bed until just before sunrise, when I heard Uncle Alex's taxi beep its horn. Oh, how I wished I were returning home with him.

CHAPTER 4

Waking to the sound of traffic and the smell of bacon and toast, I knew that Uncle Alex was not coming back to rescue me. "Not feeling too chipper this morning, are we," said Mrs. Esplen as she gave me a big hug before I sat down to eat. "I know how you feel. Both Alex and I came to UBC from small prairie towns and felt so out of place and lonely. Then we began to make friends and met each other. In fact, when I went home for the summer after the first year, everything seemed so small and I no longer had much in common with my old friends. The things I missed most, though, were the vast skies stretching across miles of prairies to the horizon and the smell of aspen and poplar trees in the spring and fall. Here you will still have the vast expanse of ocean to remind you of home, and I assume you will soon make friends. When you were at UBC, Alex copied names of drivers who are looking for people to join their carpool. Let's give them a call."

A few days later, a battered 1954 Chevrolet drove up and beeped its horn. As I walked out the door, the driver rolled down his window and called out, "Hi, I'm Gary, and the guys in the back are John and Klaus. We're all in third year and you're the first girl we've had in our carpool. What faculty and year are you in?" Over the next two years I can't remember them asking me another question, but every morning on the half-hour drive I heard all about their family backgrounds, girlfriend problems, courses and future plans. Heeding Mother's advice, I told them little about myself, not that they seemed interested. Even though they dated various girls, they never asked me out. I wasn't sure why. When I looked in the mirror or at a picture of myself, I couldn't see anything off-putting. Uncle Alex used to introduce me as "my beautiful niece." Over the years it's seemed that I lacked what the world calls "sex appeal." Small talk, sexy clothing, flirting and flattery go against my grain, and I soon learned what disasters can ensue if you compromise yourself for the sake of popularity.

What an eye-opener my first-year courses were. Although I had read extensively, it didn't compare to having Professor Gibbons read King Lear's ruminations in an old man's quaking voice, or Professor Allan engaging us in spirited and often controversial discussions about events in Canadian history. Over a thousand years of English literature and four hundred years of Canadian history came alive for me. Ever since, good literature and introspective history have been my inspiration, my guide and my support in both good and bad times.

On the other hand, most of the education courses were boring, impractical and poorly taught. Some of the instructors were former employees of the Normal School teacher training facility, which closed in the fifties. The course on primary teaching methods was taught by a blousy middle-aged former Grade 1 teacher. In a saccharine voice, she introduced herself and said, "Now, boys and girls, we are going to start by learning to properly print our letters." For the rest of the semester she continued in this vein. I soon learned that, if I showed up for the occasional lecture and read the textbooks, I could ace the exams.

Despite Mrs. Esplen's assumptions, I didn't make any friends. The girls seemed cliquey, and with my Eaton's wardrobe and shyness nobody reached out to me. When I wasn't in class I spent most of my time at the library or the outdoor pool. By December, most of the girls in my PE swimming class were complaining about the cold dressing rooms, showers and pool and were skipping classes. However, I had spent the previous years of my life swimming in the frigid Pacific waters, so seventy-degree pool temperatures were no big deal. After class I would shower, towel myself dry, squeeze the water out of my braid and, smelling like a bleach bottle, run across campus to my next class.

The library became my second home. Surrounded by thousands of books and extensive card and microfiche files, my world expanded. I would find an unoccupied carrel or plop myself down in a corner and lose myself in a world of ideas and literature. I sometimes wondered if my brain had enough space to accommodate all the ideas, information and people I was encountering. Books became a substitute for friends, but I was still lonely.

Even though I was nervous about returning to the Island without Uncle Alex to guide me, what a joyous homecoming it was to be back with the people I loved. Even Mother was more affectionate and talkative than usual. In anticipation she had filled the pantry with all my favourite Christmas food: light and dark fruitcakes, mince tarts, shortbread, cinnamon buns and much more. After the crackers had been snapped and the goose and mounds of vegetables and dressing eaten, Uncle Alex brought in the blazing Christmas pudding, and I found in my serving the coveted silver dollar. Matt was a little miffed at all the attention being given to me, but my heart was filled with happiness. I was home.

Uncle Alex was no stranger to the books and ideas that I had been exposed to in the previous months. After spending his teens in a small rural community where the usual talk in his father's general store was about farming and politics, and at the kitchen table, local gossip and events, he was more than ready to embrace the wide world that opened to him at university.

After his first few weeks, he discovered the dozens of stairs leading down the cliffs of the campus that led to Wreck Beach. He was hooked. Here was a world where, like the prairie sky, the sea seemed to stretch to eternity and the tides washed in the ocean's treasures. For months he filled his bedroom shelves and closet with the objects that Matt collected from our shores. One day his landlady complained about the unpleasant odours seeping out from under his door, so he hauled his treasures back to the sea. However, by then he realized that the gifts of the sea were inexhaustible and he didn't have to hoard them. Before he finished his first year he had decided that his future career would be in some field of marine biology.

"And now, Lass, enough about me. I sense that aside from the books and new ideas, you aren't very happy at university." Up until Uncle Alex asked me, I had tried to pretend that everything was going well, but I had never been able to fool him. The dam burst and my tears and loneliness spilled out. I told him that I had not made any friends and I felt like an outsider.

"Well, Lass, if they won't come to you, maybe you will have to go to them. When I was at UBC I joined the Newman Club, a Catholic social club on the campus. That is where I met Norah. I remember my father telling me that I had been baptized as an infant in Scotland, and that for centuries the MacLeods had been Roman Catholics. Since I wasn't interested in joining a fraternity, I thought that club might be a place where I could meet people and have some fun. Why don't you investigate it?"

From my first days at the club, I was invited to play cards and attend some of their social events. The club wasn't overly churchy, which was fine with me as I had little interest in organized religion. Although

Uncle Alex often read his Bible and we set up a chipped nativity creche under the Christmas tree, the closest we came to prayer was when Uncle intoned Robbie Burn's grace before special dinners. No attention was paid to Church dogma or rules. For us, God's love and grace were best known in each other and in the wild creation surrounding us.

During my second term, I still didn't make any close friends but at least I had people to talk to besides my landlady. In late April, after exams were over, I returned to the lighthouse. In many ways I sensed that I had changed. Now I had the confidence to navigate buses and ferries on my own. No longer was the lighthouse the only world I knew, and no longer was I content to imagine my entire future on a rocky, windswept island. There was another world that I was eager to explore and experience. Before I returned to school, I wanted to transform my image so I didn't appear out of place and time. I wanted to feel as comfortable and confident in the city as I had always felt at the lighthouse, and if I were very lucky, I might even be like Anne of Green Gables and find a soul friend, my own Diana Barry.

During our annual stay at the cottage, Matt and I bused to Nanaimo. I had my hair cut and styled, bought patterns and material and splurged on a pair of saddle shoes. After Vancouver Nanaimo seemed small and grungy, but Matt was entranced by the big city, its tall buildings, big department stores and bustling traffic. He peppered me with questions about the university, city sights and people. Unlike me a year ago, he was anxious to leave the lighthouse and get on with what he assumed was real life. When I look back on how Matt's life turned out, I am reminded of the saying, "Be careful what you ask for, you just might get it."

Although he never said so, I knew that on his lighthouse salary Uncle Alex would be hard-pressed to pay for both Matt's and my university educations. After two years I could get a basic teaching certificate, and if I wanted I could finish my degree later. With a lot less trepidation, and sporting an up-to-date hairstyle and my spiffy shoes, I headed back to Vancouver. "Say hello to Norah for me, and tell her if storm season holds off and I can get away, I might come visit you for a few days in October!" Uncle Alex called after me.

CHAPTER 5

Mrs. Esplen was glad to see me back but disappointed that Uncle Alex wasn't with me. I was curious about her relationship with Uncle Alex, but I had been well-schooled not to ask personal questions. Although I would still have to suffer through more education courses, the coming school year appeared promising. I was looking forward to classes in Canadian literature and world history and three sessions of student teaching. Last term I had enjoyed the student teaching, which was practical and informative, and I was delighted by the enthusiasm of the kids and the friendliness and advice of my sponsoring teachers.

The social life at the Newman Club was in full swing and, miracle of miracles, a commerce student named Eugene, whom I had met at the library, asked me out for dinner and a movie. His parents must have been rich because he picked me up in a shiny new black convertible. During dinner I was tongue-tied, which didn't seem to bother him. He did all the talking, telling me about his parents' mansion in Shaughnessy, an upscale residential neighbourhood south of Downtown Vancouver, and his university awards and world travels. As we sat through my first movie at a real theatre, *Cat on a Hot Tin Roof*, starring Elizabeth Taylor and Paul Newman, I was nervous and happy at not having to keep up a conversation. Arriving home, he reached across the seat and planted a sloppy kiss on my lips. At home we were not often demonstrative, reserving kisses for special people and occasions. I fell asleep thinking that Eugene must really like me. Maybe I had found a boyfriend. Looking back now, I wonder how at nineteen I could have been so naive.

For the next few weeks my heart pounded every time the phone rang. Then mid-term exams grabbed my attention and I settled down to studying. I was busy sewing a witch costume for the Newman Club Halloween party when Mrs. Esplen called out, "Laura, someone named Eugene is on the phone asking for you."

"Hi Laura, it's Eugene. Remember me? Listen, there's a party at the frat house tomorrow night. Wanna come?"

"Oh, well, I'll have to check my calendar to see if I'm free."

I was beginning to learn how to play the game. After a few minutes I picked up the phone again.

"Yes, I'm not busy, so I guess I can go. Is it a costume party?"

"God no, that's so uncool. But you can wear your best duds. I'll pick you up around eight o'clock."

The following day I skipped classes to go downtown to shop for a dress and shoes. In a new red cocktail dress and high heels, I stumbled around the house until just after nine o'clock, when I heard Eugene's horn honk. As I flew out the door, I couldn't help noticing Mrs. Esplen's look of disapproval. My resolution to be more talkative faltered when I realized that there was a couple in the back seat.

"Cat got your tongue, Laura? Say hi to Josh and Caroline. I'm dropping them off at another frat party."

We could hear the music blocks away from fraternity row. The porch at Eugene's fraternity house was crowded with people drinking and smoking. Inside the furniture had been moved to one side and couples were jiving to the latest rock and roll hits or making out on the couches.

"Wanna dance?"

"I'm sorry, but I only know how to waltz."

"Oh, that's too bad. I don't think they play waltz music at frat houses. Here's five dollars. The bar is in the next room."

And with that he disappeared. I found a chair in the corner and, every once in a while, Eugene would reappear with a drink that tasted like ginger ale. At first I was fascinated by the dancers. At home, Mother sometimes played classical dance music, and when Uncle Alex was in his cups he would whirl us around the kitchen doing what he called a waltz.

As the hours passed I began to feel miserable and abandoned. When I stood up my legs felt like jelly and I was dizzy and sick. I barely made it to the bathroom, where I threw up my supper and the drinks. Finding Eugene, I told him that I was ill and asked if he would take me home.

"Don't be a spoilsport. The party will probably shut down soon and then we'll leave. Meanwhile you can go lie down in the car."

I staggered out to the car and crawled onto the back seat. The next thing I remember was Eugene shaking me and saying, "Hey, Laura, wake up. You're home."

He handed me my coat and purse and I stumbled up the stairs to my room. I fell onto my bed and into a deep sleep. I woke with a headache and a vile taste in my mouth. My dress was crumpled and stained, and I was missing my shoes. I never heard from Eugene again, and it was only three months later that I realized what I had really lost

CHAPTER 6

After the Halloween debacle, I immersed myself in my studies. Work became an antidote, an opiate for ignoring the hurt I felt. The library became my second home and often my bedroom light shone late into the night. By the time I returned to the lighthouse for Christmas I was exhausted. Storm after storm buffeted the island, and the ocean churned up massive waves and surf that kept Uncle Alex and Matt up in the lighthouse, monitoring conditions and keeping eyes and ears open for signs of mariners in distress. Oblivious to the raging winds, I slept the hours and days away. Often I would catch Mother looking at me with concern, but, true to form, she never probed.

The day before my return to Vancouver, Uncle Alex asked me to walk with him around to island to see what treasures the storms had left on the shores. Leaving Matt to mind the lighthouse, we scrambled over slippery rocks and slimy seaweed. We found two green glass balls, remnants of fishing nets, an oar and half a dozen pieces of gnarled driftwood that Uncle Alex would make into lamps, stools and sculptures to sell to tourists in Tofino.

"Let's sit on this log for a while, Laura. You haven't seemed well since you came home. Is anything wrong?"

"No, don't worry. I'm just tired. It was a hard term."

"I'd like to go back to Vancouver with you, but being storm season I can't leave Matthew alone in the lighthouse. If you don't feel better soon, promise me that you will see a doctor. Both your mother and I are worried about you. Maybe you should let up a bit on the studies and get out more often."

Coming into the harbour, a soupy fog obscured most of the city's buildings. On the bus to Mrs. Esplen's house I could only see vague shadows of trees, and ghostly people. Everything seemed lifeless. I had always loved foggy days, the haunting call of the foghorn, the hidden mystery of the sea and the coziness of our home, where even in daylight hours our lamps and a fire cast shadows around the rooms and a beam of light from the lighthouse pierced the fog. Now the fog seemed depressing, mirroring the gloom I felt.

"Welcome back, dear. Are you feeling more rested since your holiday? How is Alex? With all the storms, I guess he is kept busy. Still, I was hoping he'd see his way clear to coming back with you for a few days. You must be tired after your journey. Dinner will be ready soon."

I soon settled back into a routine: school, library, home, sleep, school, library, home, sleep—and so the days passed. Like the weather I was often in a deep haze, putting one foot ahead of another, not knowing where I was going. Then, early one morning, feeling sick, I rushed to the bathroom and threw up. Up until then I had assumed a bad flu was causing my fatigue and nausea, but, recalling some information from the book that Mother had left on my bed, it dawned on me that I was pregnant. I hadn't had a period since October, I had sore breasts and no energy, but worse of all I had no memory of what had happened after I passed out in the car on the way home from the frat party. I made an appointment with a doctor at the UBC health clinic, who confirmed what I already knew.

"You are around three months pregnant, so your due date should be near the end of July."

Disbelief and despair numbed me, and on getting home I crawled under my blankets, half hoping that when I woke up it would all have been a bad dream. A rap on my door, and, "Supper will be ready in five minutes, dear," broke my uneasy sleep. After running a brush through my disheveled hair I stumbled downstairs. At the sight of the macaroni and cheese heaped on my plate I rushed to the toilet and threw up. When I reappeared half an hour later, Mrs. Esplen had cleared the table and was sitting on the couch.

"I'm so sorry. Forgive me. I just can't keep anything down. Maybe I have the flu."

Then I burst into tears.

"It's all right, dear. Come and sit beside me. I think we need to talk."

She put her arm around me, and I sank into the comforting presence of her ample body. "I'm pregnant."

Between bouts of sobbing, I told her the story of what had happened the night of the Halloween party.

"From the night of your first date I had misgivings about that boy. He just honked for you instead of coming to the door, and when he was an hour late picking you up for the party I was very concerned. Now I regret that I never warned you that men like him often take advantage of innocent, unworldly girls like you."

"Mother warned me about the dangers of alcohol and men, but at that time it didn't seem to have anything to do with me. How did she know? I don't know what I am going to do. I can't ask Uncle Alex for any more support, and after this how can I face him and Mother? They were so proud of me and so sure I would be successful, but now I have disgraced them. How can I ever go home again, and how can I look after a baby when I have no money, no job and can barely look after myself?"

All my doubts, fears and guilt spilled out, but when I looked in Mrs. Esplen's eyes there was no judgement, only sympathy and compassion.

"Let me tell you a story, dear. I told you before that Alex and I came from small prairie towns. His family were farmers and were not happy when he decided to go to university instead of taking up farming. They wouldn't provide him with any financial support, so for a year he worked on a fishing boat out of Tofino. On the other hand, my family, who owned our town's general store, was supportive and proud when I was accepted into pre-med at UBC. In our family history no one had ever gone to university, much less been a doctor. During our first year we became fast friends, and in the summer, when Alex went fishing, I returned home and worked in Dad's store. I dated some of the local boys, but after university life and knowing Alex, who was so handsome and full of life and dreams, they seemed dull and boring. I began thinking and dreaming about Alex, and by the end of the summer I knew that he was the man I would one day marry. Alex felt the same, so shortly after we returned to school he gave me a ring with a small diamond and said that, after we graduated and found jobs, we would get married. We often talked about our future, the jobs we would get, the house we would buy and the children we would have. For the next few months we walked about with smiles on our faces. Life was grand. When I returned home for Christmas and told Mom and Dad our plans, they were delighted. Mom phoned her friends and family and boasted that her daughter, the future doctor, was engaged to a future marine biologist. I was pleased that my parents were happy.

"Shortly after I returned to university to begin my second year, Alex phoned and said that his landlady was going away for the weekend, and would I like to come over so he would cook a special seafood dinner for me. Well, after dinner and a bottle of wine, one thing led to another, and by the time he drove me home I was no longer a virgin. With our Catholic backgrounds, which prohibited premarital sex, we felt a sense of guilt, but an empty house, a good meal and a bottle of wine helped us overcome our scruples. Afterwards we decided that, until we were married, we would be careful not to put ourselves in temptation's way again.

"Final exams were coming up, but I was so tired and nauseated all the time I couldn't concentrate on studying. Alex came with me, and, after his examination, the doctor told me that I was pregnant. Over the next week we were in shock, feeling that the plans for our future were coming apart. Still, Alex was a farm boy, used to seeing a season's work destroyed by insects, hail or drought and then replanting the next year.

"'Things will work out, Norah. I'll drop out of school for a year and get a job. After our baby is born we can continue working on our degrees. We love each other and we'll love and care for our baby together, and that's what really matters.'

"I said, 'But what will we tell our parents? Mine will be so ashamed of me, especially after boasting to everyone.'

"'Well, tell them the truth, Maggie. At first they may be shocked, but if they really care for you, they will come around.'

"When I returned home at Christmas I told my mom that I was pregnant, and that Alex and I would get married quietly when I returned to school. After recovering from her initial shock and disappointment, she said, 'Well, Norah, you are not the first girl to get pregnant before she is married. I could name at least half a dozen girls in our town who went away for six months to "help an ailing relative," or had a premature baby six or seven months after their hasty marriage. No, my girl, you simply can't have a baby at this time. If you think going to medical school would leave you enough time to look after a child, if Alex thinks he can resume his studies after a year and work, and if you think that your dad would continue to support you, you are badly mistaken. Your dad and nobody else needs to know anything about this. Next week we'll say we are going on a shopping trip to Regina, and when we come back your little problem will be solved.'

"When I look back, I realize that Mom had bullied me all my life into doing what she wanted. Although I had wanted to study music, Mom insisted that a musician's life was one of poverty and unemployment, and the next best thing to becoming a doctor was to marry one. The abortion took less than an hour, but I came down with a bad infection. When I returned to Vancouver and told Alex what I had done, he was furious. He asked me how I could kill our baby, and why didn't I trust him to work things out? I was already feeling guilty without having Alex attack me about my decision. Gradually, over the following months, we saw less and less of each other, and in April I gave back his ring. Not only had I killed our baby, I had also killed our love. Since then I have never let anyone decide who I was going to be or what I was going to do. I dropped out of medical school and, by working part time, I was able to take up my first love, music. Seven years later I met Mr. Esplen, and we were happily married for thirty-seven years. Our only sorrow was that we were never able to have children. The abortion had left me sterile."

"What happened to Uncle Alex?"

"Well, for many years all I knew was that he had dropped out of university and gone to Scotland. Then one day the phone rang, and a familiar voice said, 'Hello, lassie, it's Alex.' He had been back from Scotland for some years and was working as a lighthouse keeper on the West Coast. His niece and her children were living with him. Since then we have kept in touch."

"After Mr. Esplen died, did you ever think about getting together again?"

"Yes, for a while we did, but we were both set in our ways and knew that we could never recreate the love and relationship of our younger years, so we settled for being good friends. Now, Laura, can you see how it is possible to survive what seems like a disaster and go on to live a happy and fulfilled life?"

CHAPTER 7

"And they survived."

Those final words of a novel, whose name and author I can't remember, have haunted me over the years, as have the words of another forgotten writer who said, "Your life doesn't really begin until you answer the question, Why haven't you committed suicide?" I know of or have heard of people who, despite having experienced great losses, painful illnesses, debilitating depression and other tragic misfortunes, have survived, battered but not defeated. I have also known of people who seem to have led charmed lives which they chose to end. Why? It's a mystery.

A few weeks after my talk with Norah I made four decisions: I would not have an abortion, I would put my child up for adoption, I would never tell my family, and I would finish my education. Although Mrs. Esplen did not agree with my decision to withhold the news from my family, she said, "They love you, Laura, and will always support you. After all, as you have already probably suspected, they, especially your mother, have secrets and past sorrows of their own. But whatever you decide, I will always be here for you." I was not surprised at Norah saying this about Mother, as I always had a feeling that she was concealing secrets about her life before we came to live at the lighthouse. Often I wondered why she avoided people other than Uncle Alex, Matt and me.

Shutting out everything else I pursued my studies, determined to at least live up to my own expectations. However, when I began to feel the first stirrings of new life, I questioned my decision to put my baby up for adoption, but then common sense—one of my more positive attributes—prevailed, and I knew that I wouldn't be able to provide my baby with the security it deserved. Also, my child would never be labelled a bastard. I bought a cheap gold band for my ring finger, and when I began to show, Mrs. Esplen sewed me some loose tops. Staying away from the Newman Club, I hid myself in the library, dreading the thought I would run into Eugene, who would either ignore me or, worse yet, try to strike up a conversation.

Although I had previously enjoyed it, I was dreading the final three weeks of student teaching. I could no longer disguise my pregnancy, but my fears were for naught. My supervisor and sponsoring teacher didn't know me, and, noting the gold band, assumed I was married. Most of the kids were likeable and enthusiastic, but they were also a reminder of what I was losing.

"Look, dear, here's an ad in the Vancouver Sun from the Yukon Department of Education advertising for teachers." Even though the starting date was the beginning of September, Mrs. Esplen thought that I would have time to recover even if the baby was late. Right away, I sent in my transcripts and glowing student-teaching reports. Mrs. Esplen said, "With those marks and reports, I'm sure you will be hired."

It wasn't long before I received a reply offering me a position teaching in the elementary school in Whitehorse. I wrote Mother and Uncle Alex saying that I would only be able to come home for a week in late August, as I had to finish summer school and leave for Whitehorse in early September. Never had I lied to them before and I felt very guilty, but I also knew that many more lies would follow.

"Mrs. Esplen, Mrs. Esplen!" I yelled.

"What is it, dear?"

"My bed is wet and bloody and I'm having awful cramps."

"Oh dear, the baby must be coming."

"But it's almost a month too early."

She called a taxi, and early the next morning I delivered a six-pound baby girl at St. Paul's hospital. I watched as the sister cleaned her up, and I was permitted to hold her for a few minutes. Then she was whisked away and I never saw her again. This practice was common in the fifties, the idea being that it was not beneficial for the mother to get attached to the baby she was giving up. Maybe they were right. If I had held her longer, or fed her, I don't think I could have left the hospital alone.

Twenty years later I can still recall her little scrunched-up face, her blond-topped head and the strong grasp of her wee fingers. How can one fall in love so quickly?

I don't know if I had what is now labelled postpartum depression, but I think I cried every day for the next two months. At Mrs. Esplen's suggestion I took summer courses at university, which helped distract me from my grief. She accompanied me to the ferry, and just before I boarded she gave me a teddy bear and a card with two hundred dollars enclosed.

"Laura, I'm going to miss you. You've become the child that your Uncle Alex and I never had. I hope you will always think of my house as your second home and me as your second mother. Alex is already like the father you never knew."

I knew that I would miss my "second mother," my family and my lighthouse home, but I was relieved to be moving far away from my disgrace and loneliness. A fresh start and maybe a chance for redemption awaited me.

Everyone was happy to see me back, but Uncle Alex and Mother were disappointed that I was moving so far away. In his eagerness to go to university, Matt had applied himself to his studies and had completed three years of high school in two. He planned to do a science degree, majoring in marine biology. Uncle Alex was pleased, and said that with all Matt's experience he would have no trouble getting summer jobs as replacements for other lighthouse keepers when they took holidays. Mother said, "I don't know how Uncle Alex and I will survive with both of you gone." I just assumed that they would.

CHAPTER 8

As my plane circles over Whitehorse, I notice that in the week I've been away winter is yielding to spring. Although the distant cordillera is covered with snow and the trees are still bare skeletons, the willow branches are tinged with red and gold and there are dark patches of exposed soil. Soon we will hear the roar of the river ice breaking up and the Yukon River, which was the Klondike prospectors' highway to the gold fields in the 1890s, will continue its journey to the Bering Sea. When I flew into Whitehorse for the first time eighteen years ago, the hills surrounding the river valley were ablaze with golden aspen and the population, situated mainly on the west side of the river, was about five thousand people. Now a bridge spans the river and about twelve thousand people, two high schools, a hospital and a new housing development occupy the east bank. Takhini, at the top of Two Mile Hill, was formerly the site of an army and air force base and is now home to dozens of houses, some reclaimed from former military barracks. I remember being told that discarded mattresses from the barracks were donated to the sisters for insulation when they built additions to their first school.

Although I had been expecting to teach at the elementary school, when I arrived Sister Superior said that they needed a Grade 8 teacher for the new school across the river. The year before, Native children from outlying areas of the Yukon were brought into Whitehorse for high school and housed in a nearby hostel staffed by a lay order of workers. In May, when the river ice had melted and the weather had warmed, the kids took off and returned to their communities. In one day the school population dropped by half.

My class of girls was about half Native and half town kids. I soon sensed that the Native girls lacked confidence in this foreign environment and the town girls were unsure of how to interact with their new classmates. As well, some of them brought along the town's disdain and prejudices towards their new classmates. To bolster the Native girls' self-confidence, I boosted the marks on their first report cards to what I thought they had the potential to achieve and partnered girls from each group to work together on projects and assignments. In truth, I preferred working with the Native students. Unlike some of the town kids, they weren't riddled with teenage angst and insecurity, and were more free-spirited. I taught physical education to all the girls from Grades 7 to 10, and most of the best players on the teams were Native. As well as being strong and well-coordinated, they had great competitive spirits but weren't vicious or mean.

I missed the smell and sounds of the sea, but in time I grew to savour the wild and free spirit of the land and many of its people. In ten minutes I could be free of the confines of the town and out strolling in the hills or along the riverbanks. Often, when I was walking home from school through the woods, I would come across a group of students from the hostel sitting around a fire roasting something they had trapped. After a while they became comfortable with me and sometimes even offered me a taste of what they were cooking.

On my first trip to Whitehorse I brought the right clothing. Warmth, not fashion, was the main criteria for a Yukon wardrobe, and Eaton's catalogue had supplied almost everything I needed. I had to share a bedroom in the teacherage, which was not at all to my liking. I have always been a private person and need space and time alone. As soon as I could afford it I planned to find a home of my own.

After almost two weeks away, what a comfort it is to return home. When I left the teacherage I bought a small rundown house and acreage by the river. Over the years I have repaired and remodelled it. When he retired, Uncle Alex visited a few times and helped and taught me some carpentry skills. After his many years on fishing boats and at the lighthouse, he could fix almost anything. Even though we told her that my house was secluded, we could never convince Mother to leave the security of their isolated retirement cottage. Some things cannot be fixed.

I am fairly self-sufficient. By the end of each of our short summers, my freezer, pantry and root cellar are filled with produce from my garden, meat from my chickens and the occasional venison that I am offered by a nearby neighbour. A few years after I moved here a big husky and two stray cats appeared on my property and have never left. Mikey, Basil and Puss are good company, and Mikey barks to alert me if anyone comes onto the property. I have a few friends whom I sometimes invite for supper or see a movie with, but I have never been able to forge a deep relationship. I think people find me reserved and reticent, but I won't put myself into a situation where I might be hurt again.

I think of myself as a stoic, so it puzzles me why I have been an emotional wreck since I came back from the coast. I'm always tired and often in tears. I was sad when Uncle Alex died, but Mother's death is different. For years I had assumed we had few emotional connections, but maybe my tears are telling me a different story. Logically, how can I not have some connection to the woman whose heartbeat I listened to for my first nine months, the first person to hold me and give me the memories of my early years? Given this connection, I don't know why Mother was distant and often rejected me. Once, when I asked Uncle Alex why, he replied, "Ochs, wee lassie, sometimes when your heart is broken it also becomes frozen. Maybe when you are grown up you will understand." Maybe the answer was in the secret that Mrs. Esplen mentioned, but now that Uncle Alex and Mother are gone I will never know.

"Hi Matt. How are you doing? I haven't talked to you since Mother died."

"Oh, I guess I'm okay. Did you ever find Uncle Alex's lighthouse logbook and the other items I asked you about?"

"Oh God, Matt, I'm so sorry. Ever since I came home I've been busy with year-end reports and cleaning up and planting my garden. Mom's old suitcase is sitting in the corner. I'll dump it out and see what I packed. Give me half an hour and I'll call you back."

I'm surprised that Matt wants items from our lighthouse years. He has never seemed sentimental, and whenever we talk he always skirts any references to our years at the lighthouse. I wonder what surprises he will find when he dredges up this trove of memories.

"Yeah, it's all here, Matt, the log, Bible, some books, pictures, jewellery and Uncle Alex's old mac, which Mother had taken to wearing after he died. She would put it on, go to the beach and sit staring out at the sea. I remember her saying that it felt as if she was wrapped in his arms. If you don't want it, Matt, I would like to keep it. On rainy days like today it will come in handy. I'm just going for a walk with Mikey. Next week I'll phone you and we can make our plans for taking Mother's ashes to the lighthouse."

I have always intended to keep more in touch with Matt, but we live in opposite sides of the country, and sadly we don't have much in common. After I began teaching and Matt went to university, our visits to the lighthouse seldom coincided. The last time I saw him was at Uncle Alex's funeral five years ago. He never

Assumption

finished university or married. Over the years he drifted across the country, ending up in Nova Scotia where he works in the lobster industry. He was always so keen on marine biology, but I don't know what derailed him. I get the feeling that he is somewhat of a lost soul.

Despite its age, the mac still keeps me dry, but my hair is soaked. I wonder what happened to Uncle Alex's sou'wester. It would come in handy in this downpour. Unlike me, Mikey is oblivious to the rain streaming off his back. Every Christmas, Mother would give Uncle Alex a package of large white hankies, and I have a memory of him standing in the rain and wiping his face with the hankie he kept in his pocket. Hoping to find one of those hankies, I reached into the pocket, and instead pulled out a damp envelope with a small black cross on the back, addressed to Mother. When I got home and dried off, I opened the letter and a small piece of paper fell out. On it was written, YOU CAN COME HOME NOW, ELIZABETH. ALFRED DIED TWO WEEKS AGO. The postmark was from a small Saskatchewan town.

CHAPTER 9

"Hi Matt, it's good to see you. It's been a while."

"Yeah, the last time we saw each other was at Uncle Alex's funeral. Come to think of it, that was the last time I saw Mom. Was that three years ago?"

"No, he died five years ago."

"Was it that long? I always meant to go back, but somehow things got in the way. Anyway, with Uncle Alex gone there wasn't much point."

"How was your trip?"

"Long. I left Halifax early this morning, had a two-hour stopover in Toronto and then another two-hour bus ride here from Regina. What's the big mystery, Laura? I was planning on coming to the coast in August, but you made it sound like it was really important to come here now."

"I'm really hungry, Matt, so before I tell you what is going on, let's find a place to eat."

"Okay, I'm starved too, but this little burg looks like a place where they roll up the sidewalks early."

"I had lunch at a restaurant near the hotel and the food was decent. I booked us a couple of rooms for tonight. Are you ready to go and eat? After your long trip, I guess that you'll be ready for an early night and bed."

"Well, for a small prairie town this hotel looks fairly modern, and, as you said, the food wasn't bad, but I've had better. Do you remember, Laura, when we would go into Tofino on our summer holidays and buy hot dogs and fries for lunch and consider them exotic food? Other than the venison Uncle Alex's fishing buddies would give him occasionally, we usually ate seafood or Mom's chickens."

"Yeah, but now living up north, there are times when I'd die for a feed of fresh salmon or shellfish."

"So, what is this all about?"

"Well, just after I talked to you I put on Uncle Alex's old mac and went for a walk. It was streaming rain, and when I reached into the pocket for a hankie to wipe my face I found an envelope addressed to Uncle Alex. There was no return address, only a small black cross on the back flap. Inside was a note which said, 'You can come home now, Elizabeth, Alfred is dead.'"

"What the hell does that mean?"

"I have no idea, but Mother's postman told me that in all the years that he delivered her mail, a letter with a small black cross would arrive once or twice a year. My old landlady, a long-time friend of Uncle Alex's, mentioned once that both Mother and Uncle had secrets, so maybe the letter has something to do with them. Tomorrow we'll go to the post office and see if someone there knows anything. This is a small town, and if I know anything about small towns, it's often the postmaster or mistress who knows the town's business and secrets."

"'Morning, Laura. How did you sleep?"

"Not great. I was awake for hours thinking about and imagining what good or bad news we would hear today. Look across the street, Matt. That brick building looks like the post office."

"Greetings, strangers. I'm Maggie, the local postmistress. What can I do for you on this beautiful sunny morning? I haven't seen you here before. Are you visiting friends or family, or are you just passing through?"

"Hi, I'm Laura and this is my brother Matt. I recently found a letter addressed to my Uncle Alex MacLeod on the West Coast. It didn't identify a sender, but it came from this town and had a small black cross on the back. Would you know who might have sent it?"

"Oh, I sure do. Ever since I got this job, all of old Father Jean Luc's outgoing mail has had a cross on it, and for years I remember him sending letters to your uncle, who I was told lived around here many years ago."

"So, the priest has been around here a long time?"

"Yes, he was posted here right after he was ordained for what he and everybody else thought would be a short stay on his way up the clerical ladder. People young and old loved Jean Luc. He was smart, funny and very handsome. Even the men liked him because he wasn't a stickler about the rules. But someone, and I have my suspicions who—not many letters from here were addressed to the bishop in Regina—ratted him out and he has been here all these years. From what I heard, his big offences were to give communion to three or four divorced people and to allow a funeral Mass and burial in the church cemetery for a young Indian man who committed suicide. Anyway, the church's loss was our gain. All these years he has been a wonderful support, counsellor and friend to our little community. Many times he's given money from his meagre salary to people in need. I think the mucky-mucks in Regina forgot about him, or decided he couldn't stir up too much trouble out here in the hinterlands."

"Where can we find him?"

"When you leave here, look to the left and you will see the church spire. He lives in the manse. Oh, by the way, my name is Maggie, short for Magdalen, but stuck here in this backwater town I've never had much opportunity to be a sinner. Say hi to Jean Luc for me."

"Phew. If a customer hadn't come in we probably would have heard the entire history of the town and its occupants."

"Still, Matt, depending on what we can find out from the priest, we might need to get more information from her."

"There's the church and the house next to it must be the manse."

"Come in, come in and welcome. I'm sorry that I took so long answering the door, but these old legs don't move as fast as they once did. I'm Father Jean Luc Gagnon, the resident priest here at Our Lady of Mercy parish."

"Good morning, Father. I am Laura and this is my brother, Matt. Maggie at the post office gave us your name and said to say hi to you."

"You probably got your ears talked off, but Maggie is a kind soul who will help anyone in need. Both of you look a little familiar. Have we met before?"

"No, Father, this is our first time here. A few months ago a letter addressed to our Uncle Alex, who passed away five years ago, arrived at our mother's home on the West Coast. The letter inside was written to our mother, Elizabeth. With the help of the postmark, the black cross and Maggie, we traced the letter to you."

"Oh, mon Dieu. After all these years, Elizabeth has come back."

"No, no. I'm sorry, Father, but our mother died three months ago, just after your letter arrived."

"Oh no, that can't be true. She waited for such a long time to come home. What a tragedy! My heart grieves for her and both of you. I remember her as such a special, gifted girl, full of promise and with an enormous zest for life. How did she die?"

"Cancer, Father."

"The last time that I saw her she had just turned twenty-one, more than thirty years ago. How old are you, Laura?"

"I'm thirty-eight, Father."

"So, your dear mother must have been in her mid-fifties, young enough for her to start a new life or reclaim the old one. She so desperately wanted to come back to her hometown and her beloved prairies. So sad, so sad! And how old are you, Matt?"

"Thirty-four."

"All these years and she never mentioned that she had a son. She used to write to me two or three times a year, but as the years passed her letters became more infrequent, and she seemed sad and lonely. She mourned the deaths of her parents and was so upset that she couldn't lay them to rest or visit their graves. I thought that the news of Alfred's death would finally give her some peace and hope. So sad, so tragic!"

"Who was Alfred, Father?"

"Why, Laura, he was your father."

"My father! No, no, that can't be true. Mother always told us that our father died in the war."

"Well, all I know for sure is that Alfred was your father, but not Matt's."

"I'm really shocked, Father. And confused. It would seem that the Elizabeth you knew was not the mother we knew and that her life was a cover-up. I wonder if Uncle Alex knew."

"Yes, she had to tell him everything, because when she fled she needed him for protection and anonymity. A number of years ago, when I was researching the town's history for a book I was writing, I came across baptismal records which revealed that your Uncle Alex was your grandfather's brother. Nobody knew much about Alex, except that when he left for university he only came back once to visit his brother and family. Once, when I asked your grandmother about him, she said that after a falling out with your grandfather he went to Scotland, only returning to Canada and the West Coast after more than a decade. Elizabeth was his favourite niece and they kept in touch, and once she showed me a picture of him that she kept in her diary."

"What the hell! None of this makes sense. If Alfred wasn't my father, then who was?"

"Try to be patient, Matthew, and I will tell you all that I know. In my records there is a newspaper clipping that you should see. For over fifty years I have been recording births, marriages, deaths and town and area events. It may take me a while, but I remember the year of the fire, so that might make it easier to locate the right file. In the meantime, why don't you go into the kitchen and make yourself a cup of tea?"

CHAPTER 10

"What do you make of all of this, Laura? Does it mean that we are only half brother and sister? Does it mean that maybe my father is still alive? Does it mean that Mom lied to us all these years?"

"I don't know, Matt. It seems that nothing we assumed about Mother or Uncle Alex or even ourselves is true. I hope Father has some answers."

"I'm sorry to have kept you waiting, children, but I finally found the news clipping from our local paper dated July 28, 1944. As you can see, the headline reads, 'Local wife and daughter perish in house fire.' Do you want me to read the article?"

"Yes please, Father."

"'Somewhere between July twentieth and twenty-second, local residents Elizabeth and Laura, wife and daughter of Alfred Schmidt, perished in a devastating fire at the old homestead of Elizabeth's parents, Ronald and Ellie MacLeod. Alfred said that he had driven his wife to the homestead on July 19 and, as was her yearly routine, she intended to stay six or seven days and clean up the house and garden. When he drove back to the homestead a week later he found a scene of utter devastation. The house and barn had burned to the ground and all that remained was a huge sodden pile of ash, which had fallen into the cellar. It appeared that nothing had survived the fire. We extend our deepest sympathies to Mr. Alfred Schmidt and Mr. and Mrs. Ronald MacLeod.'

"The town was in shock. Everyone had known the families for many years. The fire was blamed on a violent lightning and thunder storm which had hit the area on the night of July twenty-first. On the prairies it is not unusual for houses, barns and sheds to be destroyed by lightning. The homestead was very isolated, so the fire had gone unnoticed. I asked Alfred about a funeral, but he angrily replied, 'There are no bodies left to bury, so what's the sense of a funeral and all that Latin mumbo jumbo?'

"Elizabeth was an only child, and her parents were devastated. A few weeks later I drove them out to the homestead, and, as Alfred had said, nothing had survived the fire. To give the MacLeods some comfort, I laid the chalice and bread on an old scorched tree trunk and celebrated a funeral Mass for Elizabeth and Laura. We made a cross out of fence pickets, laid some ashes on the ground and covered them with the prairie wildflowers which Elizabeth so loved. Over the years a wild rose bush covered the site. A week later, news came that four local lads had been killed in France and the town's attention turned to this new tragedy. Other than me and Elizabeth's parents, and maybe Alfred, I don't know if anyone else ever visited the site of the fire."

"You seemed to have known our mother well, Father."

"Oui. Shortly after I came here I gave Elizabeth her first communion. It was delightful watching her grow into such a beautiful, talented women. She could play the piano and sing like an angel. Her parents had big hopes for her future. She had many admirers, me included. If I hadn't been so many years older than her and committed to my vows, I may have joined her band of suitors."

"So why did she marry so young?"

"She met Alfred at a school dance at the end of Grade 12. He was mad about her, and when war was declared a few months later he enlisted and convinced Elizabeth to marry him before he went overseas. She asked me to perform the ceremony, and with just her and Alfred's parents and their best friends present, I married them. Her parents and I tried to convince her to wait until Alfred returned and she got to know him better, and although she was willing, Alfred was not. Three months after they met and two weeks after their wedding, he left for training camp. She didn't see him again until almost four years later. After he was badly injured in the Dieppe raid, he returned home in 1942 to find that he was the father of a daughter who, with her dark hair and eyes, was a photocopy of him. Now that I think about it, that is why you looked so familiar."

"So is my father dead?"

"Oui, and your grandparents too. After the fire your grandparents were never the same. A few years later they died of heart attacks, but I think that their hearts were broken by the death of their treasured only daughter. Alfred became a recluse, bitter and angry. He lived with his parents on their farm, and after they died the farm fell into disuse. The only time anyone saw him was when he came to town to buy groceries or liquor. People were a bit scared of him. He usually had an angry scowl and ignored anyone who tried to speak to him."

"A few months ago I got a call from a hospital in Regina. They said that a patient, Alfred Schmidt, was dying of cancer and wanted to see me. I hardly recognized him. As a result of the chemo he had no hair or beard and was gaunt and wasted. The doctor said he probably had only a few days or a week left. When he saw my collar, he whispered, 'Thank you for coming. I'm dying, Father, and I want to clear my conscience and make my peace.' He stopped, his eyes closed and I thought he was gone, but then with a big sigh and in a barely audible voice, he said, 'I killed them.'

"'Killed whom, my son,' I said.

"'I killed my daughter, my wife and her lover. She was cheating on me. I shot him and shoved Elizabeth and Laura into the bedroom and set the house on fire.'

"I was so shocked I couldn't say anything, and when I recovered his eyes were closed and he was barely conscious. I gave him absolution and the last rites, knowing that any penance that I would have given him could not have been worse than the guilt and remorse he had endured for so many years. A few days later the hospital phoned to say that your father had died. He is buried in the family plot."

"How did you know that my mother and I were still alive?"

"The spring after the fire I received a letter postmarked Tofino. She wrote that you were living with her Uncle Alex, a lighthouse keeper on the West Coast. She asked me to send her news about her parents and begged me not to reveal that she was alive or her whereabouts, as Alfred might find and kill her. Elizabeth never told me what had happened, but for all these years I have honoured her request. She gave me a post office box number in Tofino and, after your uncle retired she sent me a new address. Not knowing what happened at the homestead has haunted me all these years. I was tempted to tell Alfred that his wife and daughter were still alive, but what good would that have done? Over the many years of ministering to my people I have come to realize the sad truth that most people's sorrows and afflictions are of their own doing, and often lead to their undoing. Right now I have a parish council meeting, but if you come back tomorrow I might have more information for you."

"Good morning, Father."

"I hope you both had a restful night."

"I can't answer for Matt, but I didn't fall asleep until dawn. My mind kept trying to sort out all the things you told us yesterday."

"I didn't sleep well either, Father," said Matt. "Questions kept swirling through my head. Would you have any idea who my father was?"

"I'm sorry, but I don't. Laura, you might be interested in this picture that I found in the church files. It is dated June 23, 1943, and was taken at the church summer picnic. Do you recognize anyone?"

"The women standing next to the little girl looks like our mother."

"Yes, you're right, and the little girl is you."

"Who is the man standing next to Mother?"

"He was Alfred's cousin from Alberta. He would spend his summers at the farm, and when he grew older he would help out with chores. He and Alfred were great chums until Alfred came back from the war badly scarred and bitter towards the world."

"Father, would you drive us out to the homestead?"

"Oh Laura, other than trees, prairie and the ruins, there is nothing to see. The spring after your mother began to write to me she asked if I could retrieve a metal cookie tin from the cellar. I thought it was an odd request, but I drove out to the homestead. Of course, finding anything in the cellar was an impossible task, as it was full of ash, burnt wood, and water from the spring melt. Also, I didn't think that anything, not even a metal tin, could have survived the ferocity of the fire. Still, if you want to go, come back this afternoon. It's about an hour drive, so we should be back by nightfall."

CHAPTER 11

"Well, here we are. There's not much for you to see but vast grasslands and this abandoned homestead, but prairie folk love the landscape and skies that stretch in unbroken arcs to the horizon. Other than birdsong, the scampering of small animals and the sound of the wind rustling the leaves and grasses, the silence envelops you. Years ago I travelled to Europe and visited many of the great cathedrals, but never did I find a place as conducive to prayer and meditation as here on this vast sweep of prairie. Over there by the clumps of lilac bushes was the house. We'll have to walk, as it looks like the road has grown over since I was last here about five years ago. Until they died, your grandparents would come here every year and repair and paint the cross, weed the little mound and cover it with prairie flowers. I think they must have made arrangements for upkeep on the site, because whenever I have visited someone has repainted the cross and planted more wild rose bushes."

"I've been here before! I know this place."

"Oh, come on, Laura, you were only four years old when you left. You can't possibly remember."

"But Matt, I do, I do! I remember a big garden where I helped Mother pick vegetables and put them in a root cellar, which I hated because it was dark, musty and filled with spiderwebs. Matt, do you remember the root cellar at the lighthouse?"

"Cellar! Oh, mon Dieu, Elizabeth might have meant the root cellar, not the house cellar. Do you know where it was, Laura?"

"No, I don't, but it must have been close to the house for easy access. During a blizzard, Uncle Alex said that the farmers would tie a rope from the house to the barn so they wouldn't lose their way. Before we look for it, let's see if the cross is still standing."

"Look over there, Matthew. I see a cross in among a clump of wild rose bushes. Someone has recently painted and weeded around it. Let's sit here for a while before we look for the root cellar.

"That hole that you can see over by the lilac bushes is where the house was. Now there is nothing much to see except weeds and bits of burnt wood. I see the creek is still running. Elizabeth said that the water was sweet, unlike the water from the wells in town, which was alkaline and often foul-tasting. She and her parents would fill barrels and take them home."

"Laura, I think I found it, here on the side of the gully. The door is falling apart, and I can see stairs. Do you have a flashlight, Father?"

"Yes, look in the glove compartment."

"Careful Matt, the stairs look rotten. Can you see anything?"

"Yeah, wooden shelves holding dozens of glass sealer jars, empty bins and a dirt floor. Don't come down, Father. It's not safe."

"Do you see any tins?"

"There's a bunch on the shelves and a few on the ground. Come and help me bring them up, Laura."

"No way! This place gives me the creeps. Just hand them to me."

"Okay, but they're really rusted and grimy."

"Do you know what Mother was looking for, Father?"

"No, she just said an English cookie tin. There's seven of them here. Can you open them, Laura?"

"I'm afraid to. I might be opening up Pandora's Box. Crumbs, mouse droppings, mould and dust—but what is this? It's a diary with a rusted lock."

"Open it, Laura. What does it say?"

"The inscription reads: January 19, 1937. To Elizabeth Laura, our beautiful daughter on her sixteenth birthday. May all your days be filled with love, light and laughter, and may you bring to your family and friends the happiness that you have always brought to us. Love and blessings always, Mom and Dad."

"The first entry is dated January 20, 1937, and the last entry is dated July 20, 1944. Oh, dear Elizabeth, what is in this diary that was so important for you to have?"

"Father, Matt and I are very thankful for all for all your time and help. There is still a lot we don't know, but we'll read Mother's diary as we drive out to the coast and hopefully we'll learn more about her life and what happened to her. Before we leave the homestead, we want to inter some of Mother's ashes on the gravesite. From what you have told us, she was happy and at peace here on the farm. We will come back next summer and bring you Mother's diary to read."

"Travel safely, dear children. I look forward to your return."

CHAPTER 12

"I'm glad we picked up the car rental last night after we said goodbye to Father Jean Luc. With our early morning start, we should be in Calgary before suppertime. When you woke me this morning, Laura, the room was so filled with light I thought that it must be around ten or eleven, but here we are on the road, and although it's only six a.m., it looks like the sun has been up for hours."

"Yeah, isn't it great? During mid-summer in the Yukon, dawn and dusk are moveable feasts. I can be gardening at eleven at night or at four in the morning. In the summer, when I'm not teaching, I live my life outdoors. I have an old wood stove in my outdoor porch, and I can be making preserves or canning at any time of day or night."

"Are you happy with your life in the Yukon?"

"Well, yes, for the most part. I don't have any close friends, so sometimes I'm lonely, but my animals are good company and most days I love being surrounded by nature. After the commotion of the classroom I value the peace and solitude. Still, sometimes in winter, when the sun doesn't rise until nine and sets at three, or when a blizzard snows in my road, I think about leaving the Yukon, but in my heart I know that the only other place I could settle would be our lighthouse island. What about you, Matt?"

"Since I left the lighthouse for university there hasn't been another place that I could call home. In the last fifteen years or so I've lived in at least six or seven different places, and I'm still searching for home."

"Oh look, I see some buildings or maybe a small village up ahead. Do you want to stop?"

"Sure. I'm starved, and I really need a cigarette and a cup of coffee. Have you ever smoked?"

"No, even though a lot of kids at UBC did and most of my staff do. My addictions are books, music and sometimes travel. How did you get started?"

"At university and since then most of the people I have worked with have been smokers. I guess I followed the crowd. I always intend to stop, and now that more and more places are outlawing smoking, I just might do so."

"Look at all the trucks parked here. Maybe that's a sign that the restaurant has decent food. Let us stop here."

"Thanks, miss. I haven't eaten a breakfast like this for years."

"Yeah, well, most of our early-morning customers are bachelor farmers and they like to stoke up before starting a long day. Where are you folks from?"

"I'm from Nova Scotia, and my sister here is from the Yukon."

"Wow! You're lucky to have travelled so much. Me, I've been stuck in this burg forever. Dad says that if we don't have a drought or a hailstorm, and if we get rain, he might be able to send me to university in the city where I could board with his sister. If not I'll probably end up doing what most of the girls around here do."

"What's that?"

"Get married and have a bunch of brats. Where are you headed now?"

"A remote lighthouse island on the Pacific Coast. We grew up there and now we are taking our mother's ashes home."

"Have a safe trip. I wish I was going with you."

"These prairie girls sure can talk. If we had stayed half an hour longer we probably would have heard her and the town's history. Can you drive for a while, Matt? I'm feeling drowsy."

After four days of talking, upsetting news and noisy surroundings, it's good to close my eyes and shut out the world. All I can hear is the engine's rumble and the sound of wind rustling the tall grass. Ever since I flew into Regina, the one constant has been the wind. If I lived here, I wonder if it would get on my nerves or, like so many other things, I would just block it out.

When I arrived on the prairies a few days ago all I saw was a bleak, arid landscape, but as the days pass I am becoming aware of the vibrancy, energy and purpose of the land and sky. Everywhere I look there are signs of life. Clouds and birds skitter across the sky, gophers pop out of underground tunnels, a lone coyote paces anxiously, herds of antelope flow into the horizon and the silver green leaves of a lone aspen shiver in the breeze. How could Mother ever leave here?

"How long have I been sleeping, Matt?"

"It's nearly noon and we left the café just before nine."

"I'm really tired. All this information about Mother, my father and the fire has left me emotionally drained and with a lot more questions. Now I really have to pee. I hope the next gas station isn't too far."

"Well, there's nothing stopping you from going behind the car. I haven't seen another vehicle for at least half an hour."

"Easy for you to say. All you need do is pull down a zipper, whereas I have pantyhose, panties and a skirt to contend with. If we want to finish reading Mother's diary before we get to the coast, we had better get started. Do you want to keep driving for a while and I'll begin? The pages are damp, but considering that the diary has been stored underground for over thirty years, it is still in good shape. The embossed leather cover probably helped preserve it. When reading the dedication, you get a sense of how much our mother was loved by her parents. Being an only child, they probably had great hopes and expectations for her."

I begin to read the following:

January 19, 1937

To Elizabeth Laura, our beautiful daughter, on her sixteenth birthday.

May all your days be filled with love, light and laughter and may you bring to your family and friends the happiness that you have always brought to us.

Love and blessings always, Mom and Dad

"Matt, I've often thought it's a tragedy that most of our wishes and prayers for ourselves and others never come true. I think it's amazing that after all the millenniums of unanswered petitions, humanity still continues to hope."

"Well, maybe in the bigger picture what we get is better than what we wished and prayed for. I wonder what hopes and dreams Mother had."

January 20, 1937

Dear Diary,

Yesterday was my sixteenth birthday and I feel like I am at the beginning of a new and exciting adventure. Maybe when I am old, I'll read this diary and remember what it was like to be young. I had a wonderful birthday party. Most of my school friends, some townsfolk and Father Jean Luc were here. Besides this diary, I received a plethora (isn't that a great word) of gifts. My best friend Maggie gave me a silver charm bracelet, Donnie gave me a bottle of perfume, and Father Jean Luc gave me a St. Christopher medal on a silver chain. I also received records, books and new clothes. I felt very grown up in my new dress and first pair of high heels. Mother put my hair in a chignon and let me use her lipstick and mascara. I've got a feeling that this grownup Elizabeth is going to require a lot more upkeep than the old me. Up until yesterday, I had not been allowed to date, but Dad said that now I am almost a grownup, I can accept Donnie's invitation to go to the movie with him next Saturday. Oh, it is going to be so much fun to be grown up.

"Matt, you can just hear Mother's enthusiasm and zest for life, so different from the woman we knew. When we were growing up, did you ever wonder why we had no other family than Uncle Alex and Mother?"

"No, despite my curiosity about most things. I never questioned our situation. I assumed that most families were like ours."

"I never thought about it much either until I read Little Women, and then for some years I wished that I had sisters and a father."

"Looking back, we grew up in a bit of a vacuum. No relatives or family history to tell us where we came from or who we really were. Maybe after reading Mother's diary we'll find some answers."

February 20, 1937

Last winter the parish council bought a projector and screen and now they show a movie every second Saturday night in the church hall. People come from town and outlying farms, so movie nights often turn into party nights. After the movie, the chairs are stacked, and we dance and eat until almost midnight. Someone half jokingly suggested that Father say Mass at the end of the movie so people wouldn't have to travel home only to return a few hours later for church. Last night's movie was Mutiny on the Bounty with Clark Gable and Charles Laughton. Oh, Clark is so dark, handsome and suave, not at all like the local guys. I wish I could go to Hollywood and meet him and other movie stars like John Wayne, Greta Garbo, Fred Astaire and Ginger Rogers. What exciting and wonderful lives they must lead! Donnie picked me up and walked me home. As we were standing on the porch, I saw the front curtains move. Mom probably saw Donnie plant a soggy kiss on my lips. Ugh! I've known Donnie since we were little kids and it was like kissing my brother. I wonder what it would be like to kiss Clark Gable—not that I will ever know.

"Gee, I'm really hot and hungry, Laura. The temperature must be around ninety in the car, and more outside."

"Yeah, me too. I'm sticking to the seat and a cold beer would sure taste good right now. The last sign said thirty-six miles to the next town, so we'll stop there and find a gas station, restaurant and a shady place to eat our lunch."

"Finding a tree and a beer might present a challenge. I've never seen such a barren landscape. I wonder if the town is dry, too"

"Stop, Matt, there's a café and a gas station—69.9 cents a gallon. That's a lot cheaper than Whitehorse. You get the gas and I'll run into the café and pick up some takeout. Park the car and we can sit under the shade tree across the road"

"How is your lunch, Matt?"

"It's okay, but for the last ten years I've eaten so much restaurant food that there are times I would give my right arm for a home-cooked meal like Mom used to make."

"Yeah, even in the week before the supply ship arrived we never lacked for tasty food. Do you remember the vegetable garden that Mother hacked out of the barren soil and rock?"

"Do I remember? Every day I had to carry out and dig in the scraps and fish bones, and when the tides were low I would collect seaweed and dump it on the garden. At times it was a smelly job."

"Mom always seemed happiest when she was working in the garden or canning or making preserves. Maybe it reminded her of her prairie roots. If we leave the country roads and get onto the Trans Canada, we can probably make Calgary by evening if we don't get behind too many rigs and trailers. Shall I read now, Matt?"

"Sure. Maybe I'll snooze a little."

March 16, 1937

My second-best friend, Mavis Murray, left school a week ago to stay with her aunt who lives on a farm north of Edmonton. She said her aunt is sick and needs help to care for her children. However, Maggie told me that she overheard her parents mention Mavis and the words "pregnant and disgrace." Whenever Mavis came over, I could tell that Mom never liked her. She said that she was too fresh and disapproved of her tight sweaters and flashy jewellery. Mom likes my friends who are quiet, reserved and respectful, and Mavis,

> *although she is a lot of fun, is none of those. She has a boyfriend, Alan, the mayor's son, who is eighteen and has a car. Mom has forbidden me to ride with them, as "there is plenty of trouble around without searching for it." When I think about it, I can remember other girls who went away to help a sick relative. I wonder?*

"In that era, do you think that young girls knew much about sex?"

"Growing up in a farm community they probably knew a bit about the birds and the bees, but it was probably never discussed much, especially in relation to people. I don't think Mother was at all comfortable discussing the topic. One day when I was eleven, sanitary pads along with a pamphlet about menstruation appeared on my dresser, and just before I left for university she left a book about the facts of life on my bed. Unfortunately, I didn't read it until over a year later. Since the sixties, young people have seemed more informed and less prudish and hesitant talking about sex. Some unwed mothers are even keeping their babies. When I look back, I can't believe how naive and innocent I was when I went to university. How about you?"

"Well, I didn't even get the book and I don't know if Uncle Alex ever considered enlightening me. I did find a package of what I thought were balloons in my suitcase when I left for university. Strange going-away gift, I thought. The locker talk after my phys-ed classes was an eye opener. My first girlfriend was a flowerchild, and it wasn't long before we did it. Figuratively and literally she took me in hand, and I found out the purpose of those balloons. Since then I've been with half a dozen women, and sometimes I wonder if I have any unknown children out there. I get restless and have never been able to keep a relationship going more than one or at the most two years. "What about you?"

"Look, Matt, there's a sign for the Royal Tyrrell Museum. Do you remember seeing pictures of dinosaurs in our National Geographic magazines?"

"Yes, I used to have nightmares about them and the monsters that Uncle Alex said lived in the closet under the stairs. I think it was his way of keeping us out of the closet where our Christmas gifts and treats were stored. Now I think different fears keep us from opening closed doors. What do you fear?"

"There's another sign: Calgary, 90 miles. Shall we overnight there?"

"I was in Calgary about thirty years ago, but that was before the big oil boom. Now, from what I hear, Calgary has lots of money but little culture. Stetsons, cowboy boots and the Calgary Stampede define the city for outsiders. Still, we should be able to find a decent T-bone steak, since this is cow as well as oil-well country."

CHAPTER 13

5:00 a.m. The sun's up and Matt is still sleeping. I hardly slept all night; too much noise: trucks, cars, sirens and the TV next door. It's odd, howling winds, crashing waves and thunder never keep me awake, but those sounds seemed to fit into the natural rhythm, whereas city noises like here in Calgary are disconnected and jarring. I could never live in a city. The constant noise, hordes of people and scarcity of natural spaces leave me feeling claustrophobic, agitated and out of step with my inner self. I remember that, after two months of summer school at UBC, I could hardly wait to return to Whitehorse and my house in the woods.

Our room faces west, and in the distance I can see snow-capped mountains. Looking at them I feel uneasy and tense, the same feeling that I experienced yesterday as we drove across the flat prairie landscape. I think what I am experiencing is déjà vu, but I have never been in Alberta before. A picture keeps flashing across my mind of riding in a hot car through fields of grass as tall as the car, of tall red buildings and of someone crying. The mountains that I see out the window seem strangely familiar. I keep getting a weird feeling that I have seen all this before.

"Wake up, Matt. If we want to visit Banff and make Golden before nightfall we should be on our way. How did you sleep?"

"Great! I was out before my head hit the pillow."

"Didn't the traffic and sirens bother you?"

"Oh, hell no. For a few years I lived close to a busy rail line and got used to the constant rumble, clacking and whistles of the trains. Now, I can sleep through anything, except maybe a guilty conscience."

"What would you have to feel guilty about?"

"Well, it's a long story. Sometime I'll tell you about it. Right now I'll go and check out."

I'm glad Matt is driving, and we decide to get off the main highway and take some side roads. I like this foothill country, the rolling hills, wide open spaces, and small houses tucked among the aspen trees often beside a creek. The mountains are far enough away so I don't feel hemmed in. I could probably be happy living in this area and teaching in a country school—probably not many of those around anymore. Nowadays most country kids are bused into nearby towns for school.

"Shall I read now, Matt?"

"Yeah, go ahead, but let's stop for breakfast in an hour or so."

July 10, 1937

Three days a week I'm working in Dad's store. He is paying me twenty-five cents an hour. I've never had money of my own to spend how I please, but I'm going to save it so that when we go to Regina I can buy things which our town stores and Eaton's catalogue don't carry. I'm luckier than many of the kids at school. A lot of their parents, especially the ones who are farmers, are barely scraping by. I often see other girls wearing my hand-me-downs. Dad doesn't talk about it but one day when he was home sick I read his ledger and saw how many of his customers are buying on credit. Some debts go back to the early thirties. As well Mom keeps a big pot of soup on the stove and plenty of home-baked bread for the vagrants who come to our door. My parents are very generous, especially compared to that other Scotsman, Judge McGregor, who won't even let the tramps eat the windfall off his apple trees. Dad says the Depression won't last forever, and the farmers will prosper again, especially if that madman Hitler leads Germany into another war.

I can't imagine what it must be like not to have enough food, decent clothes to wear or even a house to live in. We didn't have many luxuries at the lighthouse, but we had what we needed. Since my university days I've always had a decent paying job and have never known want. I remember Mrs. Esplen telling me about the years when she struggled to put herself through school. She would go to a restaurant, order a bowl of soup and fill herself with the free crackers. Some days that's all she had to eat.

"Shall we stop at that restaurant just down the road?"

"Yeah, the food at the country restaurants seems fresher and tastier than the fast-food ones off the main highways."

"Good afternoon and welcome. I haven't seen you here before.'

"No, we're just travelling through on our way to the West Coast."

What can I get for you?"

"Some cold water, and then what would you suggest for our lunch?"

"The cook made perogies and cabbage rolls this morning, so they are really fresh."

"Sounds good. I've never tasted either of them. Are they local dishes?"

"No, there are lots of Ukrainians and Polish people on the prairies, and perogies and cabbage rolls are an essential part of their cooking. No celebration, especially wedding feasts, are complete without them."

"Have you had enough Matt? We should get on our way."

"Yeah, this was a great meal. I was really starved and the perogies and cabbage rolls were tasty and filling."

"Have you ever been really starved, like, not having enough money to buy food?"

"A few times. After I quit university I couldn't find work for almost a year. I was too proud to ask Uncle Alex for money but not so proud that I didn't accept food and accommodation from the Salvation Army and other charities. How about you?"

"I've never gone hungry, but there are other ways to be starved."

"I know what you mean. Did you ever want to get married and have a family?

"When I was younger I thought about it, but after living alone for so long I don't know if I could manage the loss of solitude or the freedom of making decisions without having to consider the wants and needs of another person. Having children would be great, but with no husband, and getting close to forty, I can't see that happening. Except for Mrs. Esplen, I've never told anyone, but when I was in second year university I had a baby girl whom I gave up for adoption. There isn't a day that I don't think about her and pray that her adopted parents gave her the life that I couldn't provide."

"I'm so sorry, Laura. That must have been difficult to keep it a secret and heartbreaking to give up your daughter. Did the father ever know?"

"Well, that's another story, but it's enough to say that he never knew that I was pregnant and that he had a daughter."

"I've heard that some provinces are starting to open the adoption files. Maybe you could find her. How old would she be now?"

"Nineteen, but what do you think she would feel about a mother who gave her away to strangers? Look, there's the sign for Banff and Lake Louise."

"Remember the pictures of Lake Louise in our National Geographic magazines? I was fascinated by the water's aquamarine colour and how it reflected the snow-covered mountains. When I was at UBC I thought about applying for a summer job at the lodge, but then life happened."

"Do you mind if we skip Banff? At this time of year it's probably a tourist trap. If we can find accommodation, let's stay at Lake Louise. I also remember the pictures and would like to spend some time hiking and exploring the area. Maybe we can find a church for Saturday night or Sunday Mass. Would you go with me, Matt?'

"Look, that must be the lake. With the snow-capped mountains in the background and the brilliant turquoise water, it's even more spectacular than the pictures. Let's stay at the lodge and see if we can get a room with a view."

"Wake up, Matt. If we get going now we'll have time for a hike around the lake and still make it to Golden for Mass."

"When and why did you become a churchgoer, Laura?"

"Well, my decision wasn't made hastily. Do you remember Uncle Alex going into town for Mass when we were on holiday at the cottage? He often asked Mother to go with him, but she always had an excuse, so sometimes I went instead to keep him company."

"I don't remember that."

"No, you never wanted to be inside when you could be off exploring. I was fascinated by the service—bells ringing, singing, chanting, costumes and the exotic aroma of incense. Then when I was in the hospital having the baby, the nuns were so kind and compassionate and not judgemental. Being Roman Catholic was one of the requirements for the teaching position in Whitehorse, so I thought, why not join? Mrs. Esplen was my sponsor."

"I remember Uncle Alex talking about her. Is she still alive?"

"I don't know. Over the years I gradually lost touch with her, but I will never forget her support and kindness when I was pregnant."

CHAPTER 14

"Get up, Matt. If we skip breakfast we should have time for a quick hike, and on the drive to Golden we can stop for coffee and read another entry from Mother's diary."

Sunday, August 29, 1937

After Sunday Mass, Mom cooks a big breakfast and often asks friends to join us. Today she invited sisters Maude and Ellen Lynch who do a lot of work for the church but are also the biggest gossips in town. Lately, they have been heard spreading rumours about Tom Logan who lives next door to them. I overheard Maude saying to someone at church that since his wife divorced him, Tom's garbage can is always filled with liquor bottles. He's probably drowning his sorrows in the bottle, but we suspect that he has always had a drinking problem. No wonder his wife left him for James Murray, the local mortician. Today at breakfast Maude and Ellen were strangely silent. Maybe it had something to do with Father's sermon this morning. He read the Old Testament story about David who slew Goliath with the jawbone of an ass, and then remarked, "In most communities, some people's reputations are slain by the jawbones of asses." There was a gasp, dead silence and then a titter ran through the congregation.

I'm glad Father Jean Luc is our priest. Every few months, we spend a weekend with Aunt Beulah in Regina and go with her to Sunday Mass. Dad once described her priest as "having a ramrod up his ass." His long and boring sermons are usually about regulations and hellfire and damnation. Father Jean Luc doesn't preach about doctrine or rules. Rather, he talks about love, forgiveness, kindness and generosity as the backbone of a Christian life. Unlike Aunt Beulah's priest, Father Jean Luc doesn't forbid us going to services, weddings or funerals in Protestant churches which he sometimes attends himself. Except for a few grouches who complain that he is not strict or Catholic enough, most people love and respect our priest.

"Thanks for going to church with me, Matt. I go most places by myself but have sometimes wished that I had someone to accompany me to Mass. Have you been in a Catholic church before?"

"A few times, but that was many years ago. One of my girlfriends was Roman Catholic and once she dragged me along to Mass, but it didn't appeal to me. It just seemed like a lot of Latin mumbo jumbo, with all the men and little boys wearing long dresses. Today's service was a lot different from what I remember, with even a few women participating."

"You're right, things have changed a lot since I joined the Church. Now the Mass is said in English, and some of the laity, both men and women, serve in various roles."

"Are there any women priests?"

"Sadly, no, and with the Vatican clergy, hierarchy and bureaucracy being conservative and male, I can't see the day when women will be popes, bishops or even priests."

For several minutes we continue driving in silence as Matt focuses on the road. "Even though it's summer holiday time, I didn't expect the traffic to be this heavy. Maybe we should have rented a car with air conditioning. I wonder how much of this traffic is heading for or returning from Banff," said Matt.

"One of the teachers from my school was in Banff last summer and she said the place was a zoo. Tourists clutching cameras filled the stores and sidewalks. After piling out of the tour buses, they would frantically run around snapping pictures of themselves, buy postcards and ice cream cones and then board the buses again, ready for the next attraction. Shall I begin reading again?"

He nodded and I found where I'd left off.

January 20, 1938

> *Yesterday was my seventeenth birthday and oh what a wonderful surprise I had. Mom told me that we would be leaving at noon for Regina. A visiting symphony was giving a concert at the city hall and Aunt Beulah had bought us tickets. First, we went to a salon and had our hair and nails done and then went home and donned our dressiest clothes. Later, Aunt Beulah even lent me her fur stole—kind of creepy with the two fox heads at the ends. We went to the Hotel Saskatchewan for an elegant dinner, but the highlight of the day was the concert. There is no comparison between the classical music we play at home on our Victrola and the glorious music I heard last night. Listening to Mozart's clarinet concerto struck me to the core, especially the second movement which unleashed many of the emotions and passions that I keep inside and can't express in words. I play the violin and piano (not too badly my music teacher says) but compared to the music that flowed from the hearts and fingers of those professional musicians, I am a babe*

> *in the woods. I would sell my soul to make such music. Mom said there is a new school of the arts at Banff Centre and as a graduation present, next summer, maybe I could go to the music program.*

"It's great to be spending time with you, Matt. It takes me back to our years at the lighthouse when we would spend hours and days exploring the island and the surrounding woods. I've travelled a lot during my summer holidays—Europe, Japan, Australia, the United States and much of Eastern Canada—but always alone. I don't know why I never invited someone to travel with me, but as the years passed I came to prefer my own company, and besides, most of the people I knew were busy with growing families. I would have been comfortable travelling with you."

"I would have liked that too. I had always intended to travel to the foreign countries that we read about in National Geographic. As a marine biologist I could have found jobs all over the world, but things happened and my life got off track."

"What happened?"

"It's a long story, but somehow during the last few days I'm beginning to get glimpses of what went wrong. Maybe both of us will gain some insights from Mom's diaries. After all these years, maybe I'll stop feeling like an outsider, and maybe I'll finally be able to put the past to rest."

April 27, 1938

I'm disappointed that I won't be going to Banff this summer. I've spent the last year listening to classical music and improving my musical skills. Using my spending money, I've built up a collection of records and sheet music. My favourite composer is Mozart. So much of his music is joyful and hopeful, and even with the looming threat of war I am buoyed up with his optimism. Mom and Dad are uneasy and worried about the situation in Europe and how it will affect not only our little town but also the whole country. During the last war many of the local boys and men were drafted and many never came home again. Dad said that with all the uncertainty, now is not the time to be spending money on unnecessary extravagances.

"Do you spend money on extravagances Laura?"

"Lord no. Except for travelling, I live frugally. My wants are few and usually I spend money on my needs, although I must confess I am a sucker for music and books. I grow a lot of my food, make most of my clothing, and cut wood from my own property for heating and cooking. At the lighthouse we had our needs met, and other than buying books and records we didn't want for much else."

"At Christmas dinner, do you remember Uncle Alex reciting Robbie Burn's grace? 'Some hae meat and canna eat, and some wad eat that want it, but we hae meat and we can eat, and sae the Lord be thankit.' And, as well as I can recall, we were thankful and happy."

"What about you, Matt?"

"For the most part I've lived frugally, but mostly from necessity, not choice. I have a few bucks stashed which I hope will last until I get the next job, which I know won't be in an office, store or classroom. I need open space and maybe a home where I can park my boots outside the door."

June 1, 1938

It's been cloudy all day and people, especially farmers, are hoping and praying for rain. The snow melt left the ground wet enough for the seeds to germinate, but without rain in June, July and August the crops will be stunted or die, as has happened for the last eight years. Most of the local farms are in dire straits and many farmers and their sons have gone to B.C. or eastern Canada hoping to find work. The newspapers refer to this decade on the prairies as the dirty thirties because the constant winds have stripped away a lot of the topsoil from the open fields. In our town the buildings, trees, cars and machinery are coated with dust and sometimes it is hard to breathe.

October 2, 1938

Another sparse harvest for the farmers. Even Mom's gardens have suffered from the lack of rain as the springs, ponds and some wells have dried up. Our graduating class is missing some of the boys who have left Saskatchewan to find work.

"Laura, drought was never a problem at the lighthouse. In fact it was sometimes the opposite. Some summers were so wet that I remember Mom despairing that her precious vegetables and flowers were drowning in the torrential downpours."

February 13, 1939

No school again today as yet another blizzard sweeps through our area. The snow is up to the eaves and the roads are impassable so Dad can't get to the store, not that there would be any customers anyway. Storms are also sweeping across Europe as Hitler's warmongering and persecution of Jews has people fleeing for safety. The Depression, drought, grasshoppers, dust storms, crop failures and now the possibility of war. What else could go wrong?

June 30, 1939

Yeah, I'm free! Now, that I'm eighteen and graduated from high school, I can make my *own choices. No teachers, principals, priests or even parents can tell me what I can or cannot do. I got acceptance into the music program at the University of Alberta, but Dad needs surgery in the fall and will need at least six months to recuperate, during which time he wants me to run the store. So much for being free! I'm disappointed but Dad says he will pay me, and even though I'm eligible for a $500 scholarship, it won't cover all the expenses of tuition, books, travel and room and board, which will probably be close to $1000.*

"Matt, her disappointment reminds me of that old adage, 'Man plans and God laughs.' We have plenty of time, so let's make a side trip to the Okanagan. Every summer I order cases of cherries, pears, peaches and plums from the orchards and preserve them for the winter. One of my dreams has been to park myself under a Bing cherry tree and stuff myself, or to eat a juicy golden peach still warm from the tree."

"Great idea. It must be at least 90 degrees and a swim would hit the spot. Remember how on May twenty-fourth we would dig out our swimming suits and head for the dock?"

"Yeah, I can still remember the shock of jumping into the frigid ocean and swallowing saltwater as I gasped for breath. Mother never swam, but as soon as we got out she would wrap us in towels and pour steaming mugs of hot chocolate she brought down to the dock if no one else was around."

"Uncle Alex said that as a lad in Scotland he would swim in the icy lochs. He was always a bit scared because the adults were forever warning the kids about the Loch Ness Monster. It was probably their way of assuring that the kids didn't swim too far from shore."

"I've heard tales about Ogopogo, a creature who lives in Lake Okanagan, but I think there are enough real monsters in our lives without believing in mythical ones. I wonder if Mother ever learned to swim."

"Probably not. I didn't see much evidence of water or lakes as we crossed the prairies."

"What does the next entry say?

August 1, 1939

Yesterday, we arrived at the lake and will stay until Labour Day. It will be fun to see friends that I haven't heard from since last summer. Mom is happy to be here too. Most of the husbands only come on the weekend, so their wives are not tied down looking after the whims and needs of their menfolk. After breakfast is cleared away, the older kids are set free and disappear until suppertime. My friends and I usually pack a lunch and go hiking, swimming or exploring. Our parents trust us not to get into trouble and keep away from danger. Usually we do, and if the odd time a misadventure happens, we don't tell the adults about it. When it gets dark, which is usually around ten o'clock, our mothers call us in for bed. Sometimes, after our parents are asleep, we sneak out and go for midnight swims or canoe rides or just sit and talk until the mosquitoes drive us home. Tomorrow, after Mom and I clean out the cottage and get rid of the mice and spiders, I will be free for a whole month

"Laura, I remember that feeling of freedom. After lunch, if we had finished our lessons we were set free. You were usually content to settle in with a book, but even on stormy days I couldn't wait to escape the confines of the house and go exploring. Did you miss not having friends to hang out with?"

"Occasionally, but most of my friends were my books, our dog and cats and you and Uncle Alex. Maybe if I had socialized with friends my age I would have fit in better at UBC."

August 9, 1939

I'm determined to take full advantage of this month of freedom. For the next half dozen years, I'll probably have to work in the summers to pay for university. Not all the old gang are here. Some of the kids are working or have already left for university or Normal School. There is a rumour that war may soon be declared, and even if there's no draft, many of the boys are anxious to take a swat at Hitler's huns. They think it would be an exciting adventure to go overseas. I hear the guys talking about which branch of the armed services they would like to join. I can't imagine that these guys who have only travelled our small lakes and ponds in canoes and rowboats crossing the ocean in warships or submarines. Mom told me that may of the older people in our area lost sons, husbands, fathers and brothers in the last war. She is almost glad that I am an only child.

August 14, 1939

I'M IN LOVE! Last week at the community hall Saturday night dance, Alfred Schmidt, who was a year ahead of me in school, asked me to dance. A lot of the girls at school have massive crushes on him, me included. He is movie-star handsome, another Clark Gable. He had his choice of the more popular girls, so why he picked me is a mystery. As we glided around the dance floor to the music of Benny Goodman and Glen Miller, I couldn't help noticing the envious glances of girls sitting in chairs lined up against the walls. Since the dance he seems to be everywhere I am. Tonight, we went for a long walk along the lake and he kissed me, my first kiss since that soppy one on my first date. I'm still trembling. Who knew that love could consume you so completely?

"Have you ever been in love, Matt?"

"Yeah, four or five times, but it never worked out. After a few months, or in some cases years, the flame died and I moved on. The endings were always messy, with harsh words, tears and threats, so in time I figured that being in love was more trouble than it was worth—although, there was one woman . . . Still, when it comes right down to it, I'm not very good at relationships."

August 25, 1939

Yesterday, we had our first fight. Alfred wanted to go farther than I would let him, and he stormed off saying that I was a teasing prude and there could never be anything between us. Unlike me, he doesn't believe our church's teaching that sex outside of marriage is a mortal sin, but then I have not seen him in church for years. Still, I can't stop missing him and crying. Mom says it's probably for the best. "He's too into himself and the gossip is that he has inherited his father's temper and taste for the bottle." I don't care, I don't care, I just want him back. In three days, we return home and I wonder if I will ever see him again.

"I can identify the anguish she was feeling. When Eugene, my baby's father, dumped me, I thought my world had ended, but having survived the aftermath of that brief encounter I assumed that I could survive almost anything."

"I guess we're like those people that Uncle Alex and I used to rescue when their storm-driven boats crashed upon the rocks—battered and bruised but still alive."

September 9, 1939

Today, Britain and France declared war on Germany. Neville Chamberlain, the British Prime Minister, said that although he had tried to appease Germany by ceding the Czechoslovakian region of the Sudetenland to them, their invasion of Poland was the last straw. Everyone is tuned to their radios and the evening air is punctuated by the sound of cap guns, air rifles and "bang, bang, bang" as the kids run around playing war against imaginary Germans. It's all a big game to them, but the adults are sombre and looking at their grown sons with apprehension.

"You know, Matt, I've often thought how lucky we are that, since World War Two ended, Canada has not had to go to war. I can't imagine how heart-rending it must have been for women to see their male relatives leave for the European battlefields knowing they might never see them again."

"During a difficult time in my life I was tempted to fight in the Vietnam conflict, but before I could enlist a truce was declared."

"Well, I'm sure glad you didn't go. You're all the family that I have left. Do you want to drive and I will continue reading?"

Assumption

September 11, 1939

Today, Mackenzie King joined many other Commonwealth countries in declaring war against Germany. There are long lineups at the recruitment offices, and I've heard rumours that 15-, 16-, and 17-year-old boys are lying about their ages so they can enlist. Mom and Dad just came home from a wedding reception in Regina and they said that when someone ran in to tell the guests that Canada had declared war, many of the men, including the groom, ran out, heading for the recruitment office. "Mind my words," Mom said, "there will be many tears and broken hearts before this war ends." "No, no," said Dad, "the politicians and military leaders are saying that this war will be over before the new year."

"So much for the pundits! I remember reading that, at the beginning of the war, President Roosevelt said he would not send his country's sons into what was basically a European conflict. However, three years later when the Japanese attacked the naval fleet at Pearl Harbour, the Americans not only declared war on Japan, but also on Germany."

September 20, 1939

Alfred appeared at our door today dressed in an army uniform and carrying flowers.

He started to cry as he apologized for his harsh words and abrupt departure. He said that he really loved me and would die if we couldn't be together forever. He leaves for training camp in two weeks along with most of our school chums. Some of the boys had to stay back as they are needed on their parents' farms to harvest the crops. Alfred's parents are also farmers and he is their only child, but he feels it is his duty to serve his country. After he left, Mom didn't say much but, noting her pursed lips, I could tell that she wasn't too pleased that Alfred was back in my life. Later, I overheard Mom say to Dad, "Duty! Bosh, what Alfred really wants is to escape his abusive father. Still, his staying would probably not do much for the farm. Before Schmidt bought it, the farm was productive, but he is a lazy farmer and it would take ten Alfreds to restore it to its former state."

"Matt, I remember Mrs. Esplen telling me that, in the dirty thirties, hardly a day passed that she didn't have someone at her door asking for food. Many of the hobos were prairie farmers who had lost their farms because of the long drought and the Depression. When war came, many of the drifters enlisted and some died in Europe, never to benefit from the prosperity that ensued during and after the war."

September 27, 1939

Alfred and I are spending all our time together before he leaves. Tonight, he is taking me out to dinner and then to see Wuthering Heights. I wonder if he would have come back if war hadn't been declared.

September 28, 1939

Last night Alfred asked me to marry him before he is shipped overseas. He said that he wants to have something to hold on to, something to hope for and someone waiting for him if and when he comes home. Marry. Marry? I've never imagined or thought about marriage until I at least finished university. I don't want to end up like so many of the women in this town, stuck cooking, cleaning and looking after a bunch of kids. I want to travel, have a career and meet all sorts of people with all sorts of ideas. I told him that I would think about it.

"I know how she felt. In all my relationships the women wanted a commitment to marry and have kids. Settling down wasn't on my agenda. I liked the companionship and sex, but I also liked the freedom to pick up and move when I got restless. I certainly didn't want to be tied down with kids."

September 30, 1939

Alfred said the time was getting short if we were going to marry before he left. He said, "If I get killed, at least I'll die knowing that I have been loved by the most gorgeous woman in the world. While I'm away, you can go to university, and when I return we'll travel all over the world together. Maybe one day we'll make beautiful babies."

October 7, 1939

We haven't told our parents yet because I want to talk to Father Jean Luc first. Alfred wants to get married at the town hall, but I couldn't do that to Mom and Dad. As it is, the wedding won't be the one that Mom has been planning since before I was born. Also, I want the Church's blessing on our union. Unlike Alfred, my faith is important to me.

October 15, 1939

Tomorrow is the big day. Father Jean Luc advised us to wait until Alfred comes home, and Mom and Dad are opposed, saying that I am too young and haven't known Alfred long enough to make this important decision. But I'm not too young! I always assumed that by the time I was eighteen, I would be mature enough to make my own decisions. Still, it won't be the fairy tale wedding that I had anticipated sometime in the future. Father will marry us in the morning, and only our parents and a few close friends will attend. Mom and Dad will host a wedding brunch at our home, and I will wear my graduation dress. Jenny said she would make me a silk flower bouquet. I would have liked fresh flowers, but we had a hard frost two weeks ago and the garden flowers are finished. I don't know if I will be able to sleep tonight. I'm excited but also a little scared because I don't know much about sex. Mom has never discussed the subject and it's not something that I talk about with my girlfriends. Sex seems to be a mysterious secret, although I've picked up enough clues from books and movies to think that it must be a glorious experience. Mom and Dad's wedding gift is a week honeymoon at a fancy hotel in Regina.

"Glorious? I wouldn't know about that. I was passed out for my first and only experience with sex. What do you think, Matt?"

"Oh my God, Laura! Are you saying that your pregnancy was the result of rape? Did you tell anyone?"

"Only Mrs Esplen, and that was only after I realized that I was pregnant. At that time rape was considered a disgrace, more so for a woman than a man. If possible, it was kept a secret and the perpetrator wasn't usually charged or even held accountable."

October 21, 1939

I think that I have made a huge mistake and I can't stop crying. Alfred just stormed out, probably to the bar. For the third time today he wanted sex and I said that I was too sore and tired. He called me a frigid bitch just like his mother. I can't believe this is happening to me. Our wedding night was a disaster. We had no sooner got into our hotel room when he pulled off my clothes and climbed on top of me, no caresses, no tender words, no kisses—just sex. It hurt so much, but he just rolled over, smoked a cigarette and went to sleep. He said that now we are married, we don't have to do all that mushy stuff. For the last four days, all he wants to too is have sex and drink. Except to eat we have hardly left the room.

October 27, 1939

Thank God we're home. Alfred leaves for training camp next week and I can't say that I'll be sorry to see him go. Dad's operation is next week so I'll be busy working in the store and helping Mom look after him when he comes home. Mom hasn't said anything, but I can tell by her sympathetic glances that she knows our honeymoon didn't go well and that I'm unhappy. I made the choice to marry Alfred, and for now I'll have to lie in the bed that I made. It is too soon to anticipate the future, but it can't and won't be like this past week, of that I am sure.

"Matt, how horrible and disappointed she must have felt! She probably didn't have any idea of how to remedy her mistake. Living in a small, mainly Catholic community, she knew that divorce would bring scandal and disgrace upon her and her family. There were probably families in the area who stayed together because they feared being outcasts or the women feared being destitute if they left unhappy or abusive marriages. Today, I've read that almost fifty percent of marriages end in divorce. I know that the Catholic Church doesn't allow divorce, but I can't believe God would want people to stay in dysfunctional relationships with no chance of finding happiness with someone else."

"Look, Laura, that must be Lake Okanagan. I wonder how big it is. One of the things I love about oceans is that you can sail for days with only the horizon in view. For a time, everything and everybody that you left behind disappears and you are completely free."

"Do you want to stay here for a few days, Matt? We could finish reading the diary and then head for the coast."

"That's a good idea. I'm more than ready to swim and relax on the beach. Most of all, I hope we can finally find out more about my father and why we ended up living at the lighthouse."

CHAPTER 15

November 12, 1939

Dad had his surgery yesterday and it went well. He will be in hospital for at least ten days, but the doctor said that it would likely be three or four months before he is able to return to work. By next fall I should be able to go to university. I can hardly wait, because already the store and our town are beginning to feel claustrophobic and boring. Working in the store confirms my decision to pursue a career in the bigger world. Freedom when it comes will be even sweeter since I'll know what I am escaping from.

"Laura, that's also how I felt when I left for university. Much as I loved the island, I couldn't see spending my life as a lighthouse keeper on a deserted rock. I thought that when I left, my life was just beginning. I loved everything about Vancouver and the university—the masses of people, the vitality, the opportunities, and even the noise and crush of traffic."

"I sure didn't feel that way. In Vancouver I always felt like an outsider. Even though I loved the island, after I had the baby I felt uneasy and guilty whenever I went back. Keeping my secret and my feelings to myself put a distance between us. I couldn't bear the thought of their disappointment if they found out what had happened. Now, knowing Mother's secret, I wonder if they would have understood and if I may have had a closer connection with Mother."

November 29, 1939

Today, a postcard arrived from Alfred saying that he would probably be shipped overseas before the holidays and that he was looking forward to seeing some action. There were no words saying that he missed me but only asking that I let his mother know in case she wanted to send him a Christmas package before he left.

"This may be hard for you to hear, Laura, but the more I learn about Alfred, the happier I am knowing that he was not my father."

"I have no memories of him. After knowing the pain that he inflicted upon Mother, I don't regret that I didn't see him before he died."

December 21, 1939

Christmas won't be very merry this year. So many of the men are gone and their wives are struggling to keep up their farms, businesses and homes. A spirit of lethargy has settled over the town, and everyone including me is feeling worn out. Having the last name Schmidt doesn't endure me to some of the townsfolk. Alfred's parents came to Canada just after the First World War, and Mom says that they were harassed and excluded. Over the years they kept to themselves and only came to town to shop. Last summer a nephew who teaches in Calgary came to work on the farm during his summer holidays. You would never know that he and Alfred are cousins. Alfred is tall, burly and dark-haired while his cousin is shorter, slender and fair-haired.

January 16, 1940

Another postcard. "I'm in England but not allowed to say where. The weather is cold, damp and miserable but that doesn't stop the bosses from sending us out on daily manoeuvres. The food is tasteless, often overcooked and usually cold. Via Red Cross, would you send me a wool sweater, scarf and socks and some decent food.

Cheers, Alfred

January 17, 1940

Not knowing if his parents had heard from him, Mom and I drove out to the Schmidt farm to tell them Alfred's news. Everything seemed dilapidated, including Mrs. Schmidt, whose clothes were well worn and who sported a black eye and a large bruise on her cheek. Alfred's father left as soon as he said a brusque hello, but Mrs. Schmidt invited us in for a cup of tea. Everything inside was old and worn and the house was dark and musty. It's no wonder Alfred was anxious to leave such a joyless space.

January 18, 1940

Because I've been feeling nauseated and tired for the last month, I went to see Dr. Harrison today. After examining me he said, "Congratulations, Elizabeth, you're about three months pregnant." I looked at him in horror and then burst out crying. When I stopped sobbing, I told him the story of my disastrous marriage and honeymoon. "I wish that I had seen you before you got married Laura. I would have told you about using protection." "But doesn't the Church forbid that?" I said. He replied, "If all the Catholics in town obeyed that edict, there would be many more large families around. I would have warned you against marrying Alfred. He's been damaged by growing up in a violent and abusive family. As they say, like father, like son. His mother has been so intimidated and broken down that she couldn't protect herself, let alone Alfred."

January 19, 1940

I don't know what to do. Right now, I don't want a child, especially Alfred's child. A baby should be conceived in love, not lust. The baby is due in July, just about the time that I would be getting ready to leave for university. I have really messed up my life and future.

January 20, 1940

I told Mom and Dad that I'm pregnant and they are just as distressed as I am. After a while Dad said, "We've survived a World War and a depression and drought, and if we all pull together we'll survive this. If not this fall, we'll figure out some way for you to go to university after the baby is born. Now more than ever you will need a profession to support yourself and the baby. We Scots have always been a resourceful and determined people." None of us seem to see Alfred as

> *being part of this plan. Without being told they know my marriage is a failure.*

"Matt, I wonder if I had told Mother and Uncle Alex about my pregnancy, would they have been as supportive as our mother's parents?"

"Of course they would have, Laura. I always knew that even though they seldom expressed their feelings they loved us deeply, and would always be there for us. Like his brother and her parents, Uncle Alex and Mom were also stubborn, resilient Scots."

CHAPTER 16

April 3, 1940

I'm beginning to show and it's weird how some old ladies keep patting my tummy. I think they are nostalgic, remembering halcyon days when they were new mothers. Mom said, "Time has tempered their memories of sleepless nights, piles of dirty diapers and crying, colicky babies."

May 15, 1940

My friends held a baby shower for me today. Many of them are in my situation, pregnant with husbands overseas. I wonder if some of their husbands also coerced them into marrying. I received lots of baby clothes, which is good because I haven't had the heart to make or buy them. My pregnancy still seems like a dream (nightmare is a more accurate term), but I guess I can't ignore the baby's existence any longer.

"Before my baby was born I knitted an outfit and Mrs. Esplen crocheted a shawl. I wanted my baby's adoptive parents to take them home, and I hoped that when she grew up they would give them to her so that maybe she would know that her birth mother loved her. I wonder if that happened."

June 24, 1940

According to the newspaper and radio reports, the situation in Europe is dire. France and the lowland countries have surrendered, and the German air force is blitzing England with continuous night and daytime raids. In response to the air raid sirens people are seeking shelter in the underground railway stations and their basements. In London hundreds of people have been killed when their homes were bombed, and many children have been evacuated to the countryside and Commonwealth countries. It's hard to believe, but it's a possibility that England may fall. On June 4, in a stirring speech as reported by the Leader-Post in Regina, Prime Minister Winston Churchill said, "We shall go on to the end. We shall fight in France, we shall fight on the seas and oceans, we shall fight with growing confidence and growing strength in the air, we shall defend our island whatever the cost may be, we shall fight on the beaches, we shall fight on the landing grounds, in the fields and in the streets, we shall fight in the hills, we shall never surrender."

June 29, 1940

I wrote Alfred last month to tell him about the baby but have not even received a postcard in response. I don't think he will be pleased with the news. Surprisingly, Mrs. Schmidt is excited to be a grandmother. She said that she had always wanted more children, especially a daughter, but her husband said that he didn't need another mouth to feed.

July 2, 1940

Our town is in mourning. Twenty-three Canadian pilots have been killed in the Battle of Britain and two are from our community. So far there has been no news of casualties from Canada's infantry divisions. We had hoped the war would end in months, but the conflict is engulfing most of Europe and beyond, which portends a long, drawn-out war.

July 8, 1940

It's blazing hot and I am feeling very uncomfortable. My back and legs hurt, my feet are swollen, and the baby is over a week late. Thankfully, Dad is back at the store so I can stay home. Mom and Dad gave me a crib, which I put in my room. It's crowded, but in their small house there is no room for a nursery. Alfred slept on the couch for a week before he left.

Elaine and Donna dropped by today with their new babies who were fretful because of the heat. They told me horror stories about their labours and deliveries, almost as if they had barely survived a great ordeal. Mom said not to pay any attention to their tales. "I remember my friends telling me similar stories when I was pregnant with you, but I thought if birthing was as bad as they described, why did women go on to have multiple children? Even after you were born I wanted more children, but after three miscarriages it was not to be. Despite the circumstances your dad and I are looking forward to being grandparents."

"Lordy, it's hot, Matt. I'm going for another swim to cool off. Lake Okanagan is way warmer than the ocean ever was. Even at the lighthouse, the water temperature didn't change that much from winter to summer."

July 9, 1940

I wish we could go to the lake for a swim and cool off, but with the baby coming any day now that's not possible. I've heard that some prairie lakes are so saline that you can't keep your legs under water when you float on your back. Our lake has leeches, and at the end of a hot summer you can get the itch.

I'm writing this sitting in the shade of our huge Manitoba maple tree. Mom said that it was a sapling when they moved into town from the farm fifteen years ago. I'm sewing the last of the diapers, four dozen in all. How can one small baby pee and poo so much?

CHAPTER 17

July 18, 1940

I've named her Laura Elizabeth after myself and Mother. She arrived on July tenth weighing eight pounds eleven ounces, a bonny baby, as Mom says. She has dark hair and long dark lashes and seems quite robust. I haven't really gotten to know her yet, as they only bring her to me to nurse and then whisk her back to the nursery. Dr. Harrison says I can go home tomorrow, which is none too soon. I've been in hospital for eight days and they made me stay in bed until two days ago. I can't wait to sit under the maple tree, drink cold lemonade and eat some decent food. Dr. Harrison told Mom to bring me some stout, as it is good for nursing mothers. UGH!

August 31, 1940

Yesterday I took Laura for her six-week checkup. She has gained four pounds and seems much more aware. She is always looking around and stares at me with such intensity that it feels like she knows what I am thinking. She sleeps five to seven hours at night and hardly ever cries. Mom says babies should cry as it strengthens their lung, so what am I supposed to do—pinch her?

Up until now Mom has done Laura's and my laundry. Even with a wringer washing machine it is not an easy task. Mom says that when we lived on the farm she had to haul and heat the water, and instead of an agitator she had to use a scrubbing board. Compared to those days, laundry now is a piece of cake. Still, starting tomorrow I will take over the job.

September 7, 1940

Today, Laura smiled for the first time, or maybe it was just gas. She is such a quiet, solemn little thing. She loves lying on a blanket under the maple, looking and cooing at the birds. Last night our first frost decimated the tender vegetables and flowers. Mom has been canning and pickling everything in sight, so we will be well fed this winter. Even before the war, many fruits and vegetables were not available in the winter. Mom has planted the potatoes and root vegetables at the farm, and in October we will store them in the root cellar.

Alfred's cousin came by to say goodbye before he heads back to his teaching job in Calgary. Because of his game leg and limp, he couldn't enlist. He is quite taken with Laura, and brought her a teddy bear and a book and told her not to forget him before he comes back next summer.

September 19, 1940

The nights are frosty, and the leaves are changing colour. I love the sight of the golden birch and aspen against the backdrop of a brilliant blue autumn sky. Last Sunday Dad, Mom, Laura and I drove to the farm. After we swept out the dead flies, spiders and other creepy-crawly things in the house, Dad put up the storm windows.

Dad said, "We've left the farm to you, Elizabeth, so never will you be without a home. The land is rented out, and as the economy improves it will provide you with some income. The house needs repairs, but it's liveable and soon the government plans to bring power to this area. Even before the depression we couldn't make a living here, so we moved into town, and with an inheritance from our parents in Scotland we were able to buy the store. However, times are changing, and when our boys return there will be a demand for productive farmland."

October 18, 1940

The nights are closing in and by suppertime it's pitch-black outside. Most of the trees and bushes are bare. One of my favourite autumn outings is walking in the woods, stomping on crunchy leaves and inhaling the scent of fermented berries, and leaves exhaling their last breaths. When I was small Dad would rake the leaves into a big pile under which my friends and I would bury ourselves. Now, in the early mornings and evenings, Dad says he can feel winter in his bones.

"Remember, Matt, how at the lighthouse and in Vancouver we slid easily from one season into another? Usually there was no abrupt change in temperature, and except for the rare snowfall the land remained green. When I moved to Whitehorse I found it hard to get used to the sudden transition to winter. One week you're outside in a light sweater and jacket and the next week you're wearing parkas and mukluks or snow boots."

Assumption

November 3, 1940

Today, Father Jean Luc baptized Laura. Her christening dress is very old and fragile. Mom brought it from Scotland and both she and her mother and grandmother wore it. Laura was so good. She didn't even whimper when Father poured water on her head and placed salt on her tongue. Dad and Mrs. Schmidt stood up as her godparents. Mr. Schmidt stayed away, saying he didn't have much use for priests or religious ceremonies.

December 22, 1940

Again, Christmas will be bleak this year. Many families are mourning their men killed or wounded in England and Europe. People are hoarding food, expecting that when rationing comes things like sugar, coffee, butter and meat will soon be in short supply. Although we won't be having Christmas puddings, mince pies or shortbread, we will still be better fed than many people. Mom has purchased a big turkey from a local farmer and has invited ten less fortunate people for Christmas dinner. Father has asked if Laura can be the child in the manger at midnight Mass. At sixteen pounds, it will be a tight fit.

CHAPTER 18

January 11, 1941

We were hoping that the war would soon be over, but that seems highly unlikely as the conflict is escalating with reports of increasing casualties. There are rumours that Jews are being persecuted and rounded up all over Nazi Europe, but as of now, no one seems to know their fate. In 1939 the Canadian and American governments refused to grant asylum to a boatload of a thousand Jews, and they were sent back to Europe. I wonder what happened to them.

"Until I went to UBC, I never knew anything about the Holocaust. When I saw the pictures and heard the stories about the concentration camps, I was horrified and could hardly believe that a supposedly highly civilized people like the Germans could commit such atrocities."

"I wonder, Matt, how much Uncle Alex knew. He had a radio, spent time in Tofino and read newspapers and magazines, so he couldn't have been completely in the dark."

February 1, 1941

Another postcard arrived from Alfred asking for us to send him more supplies, but with no questions or comments about his new daughter. He is disgruntled because his unit has not yet been sent to Europe. The postcard showed pictures of English pubs, which is where he probably spends his free time and money on the local girls.

April 16, 1941

Dad had a relapse, so I am back at the store. When I come home in the evening I try to take over most of Laura's care. After helping prepare dinner and doing the laundry, I fall into bed exhausted. I don't have much time or energy left to write in my diary.

May 20, 1941

Laura is crawling and almost walking now. She is a good little tyke, but we must keep her in sight as she is very curious and wants to taste and touch everything. Bedtime is our favourite time together. I read to her and one book is never enough. "More book, more book, Mama." Often I doze off before she does. Every day she is looking more and more like Alfred's daughter, which delights Mrs. Schmidt, who remarked, "If I ever had a daughter, I hope she would resemble Alfred." Although she may resemble her father, fortunately she has my and not his temperament.

June 25, 1941

Great news! Dad's brother Alex is coming for a visit. Dad has hardly heard from him since they had a disagreement and Uncle Alex left for Scotland. I've seen pictures and have heard stories about him for years and now I will get to meet him. He is a lighthouse keeper on the West Coast so will probably have exciting tales to tell.

"Uncle Alex never said anything about having family in Saskatchewan. Maybe he broke his family ties to protect Mother. She was probably terrified that if Alfred found out that she and I were still alive, he would track us down and kill me and maybe Laura," I said.

"That would explain why Mom was always wary of strangers, whether at the lighthouse or the cottage. How dreadful it must have been for Mom to live her life in constant fear."

July 29, 1941

Uncle Alex has come and gone, but it was a wonderful two weeks. Laura was enthralled and followed him around like a puppy dog. For the first week I sat and listened as he and Dad got caught up on the past thirty years. After he returned from Scotland he worked his way across Canada, ending up in Tofino and working on fishing boats. Eventually he secured a position as a lighthouse keeper on a remote island off the coast. One day he asked me why my parents and I don't talk about Alfred. "Isn't he pleased, and doesn't he miss his beautiful wife and daughter?" I couldn't contain my sadness and anger any longer and burst into tears. After I told him about my disastrous marriage, he said, "There, there, lass, nothing is ever so bad that it can't be fixed. For now, carry on as you have been doing, and when this war is over, and if Alfred comes home, you can decide what to do. Before I leave, I'll give you the information you will need if you ever have to get in touch with me."

August 3, 1941

Laura was bereft when Uncle Alex left, but now she has a new best friend. Alfred's cousin has Sundays free and spends the day in town. After Mass Mom has been inviting him back to the house for the day and sometimes supper. He dotes on Laura and she is constantly begging him to read to or play with her. Dad is pleased to have another male around, and someone to help him with chores. Michael said that sometimes he gets razzed because he isn't in uniform, and one time a white feather was left on his dashboard. When the war is over he wants to teach overseas and travel the world.

August 25, 1941

Today we drove to the farm to collect water from the creek. It has been one of those perfect prairie days, with the temperature around eighty and a soft wind rustling the wheat and barley stalks. Laura was excited to be going for a car ride. With gas being rationed, the car sits more on the driveway than on the road. We've had enough rain this summer, so the heads of grain are full and the bushes and trees on the farm are flushed with colour. I love coming to the farm in late May when the lilac bushes around the house scent the air and the wild roses overrun the yard. We filled a dozen containers with clear, cold water and I picked a bouquet of colourful wildflowers. For the first time in a long while I felt perfectly content—no thoughts of dashed expectations or unfulfilled dreams. Why couldn't Alfred have been more like his cousin?

September 3, 1941

Yesterday, Michael came to say goodbye. He picked Laura up, swung her around and, turning to me, said, "Take good care of yourself and this little treasure until I return next summer." I will miss Michael. I love Laura, but at fifteen months she doesn't provide much companionship. Mom and Dad spoil her with things they couldn't provide for me during the Depression, and I hope that she will always be cared for and well loved.

"*Stop*, Matt. Did you say Michael? That was the name Mother was calling when she died. Do you suppose that—"

"Oh, for heaven's sake, Laura. Michael is a common name. There were probably dozens of Michaels around in her town. It's getting late, so shall we continue reading in the morning?"

November 11, 1941. Armistice Day

Hundreds of people from town and the surrounding farms gathered at the cenotaph to honour and remember the dead and injured from this and the last Great War. Veterans festooned with medals, some of whom using crutches or wheelchairs; mothers, some of them widows; children; family and friends; all wore sombre faces, and many were in tears.

> *There are few people in our area who have not been touched by war. For as long as I can remember, I have been coming to these ceremonies, hearing the bugle play. The Last Post, the bagpipes droning Flowers of the Field and the school children reciting or singing In Flanders Fields. Fittingly, the weather is bleak, often with falling snow. Conspicuous by their absence are the German farmers and families, many of whom emigrated here after WWI. I wonder if they honour their war dead.*

"Matt, do you remember every year listening to the Armistice broadcast from Ottawa? Uncle Alex said that he had lost some friends in the First World War, and that it was important that he remember them. In Whitehorse, Remembrance Day is always bitterly cold, but still most people show up for the ceremony. Many of the Natives, some volunteers, some conscripted, were either injured or killed in the wars."

> *December 8, 1941*
>
> *As we walked to church this morning, people kept stopping us and asking if we had heard that the Japanese air force bombed Pearl Harbour this morning. Hundreds of people have been killed and much of the American fleet has been destroyed. Since Japan is Germany's ally, people are speculating that*

President Roosevelt will soon declare war against both countries.

December 15, 1941

Uncle Alex has sent us a message saying that the lighthouses have been put on full alert and have been instructed to watch for any signs of Japanese ships or submarines. Between the winter storms and the surveillance, he is not getting much sleep.

December 21, 1941

Everybody has been issued ration books for meat, sugar, butter, tea, coffee and gas, most of which have already been in short supply since shortly after war broke out. Mother made a Christmas cake with dried berries that we picked last summer and has hoarded some butter for baking. A farmer is trading us a turkey in exchange for groceries from the store. The store's stock is way down, but we are still better fed than most of our friends.

January 29, 1942

Work, work, work, that's all I seem to do. Mom has gone to Regina to look after Aunt Beulah, who has been diagnosed with breast cancer and will have a mastectomy in two days. Dad is still not well enough to return to

> *the store full time, so it is my responsibility to look after the store, house, Dad and Laura. I was taking her to work with me, but when Mrs. Armstrong offered to babysit I accepted with much relief. Mrs. Armstrong said that Laura's vocabulary is far more advanced than that of most children her age, and she is already starting to recognize and sound out words in her books.*

"See, Laura, even at two years old you were smart. It used to really bug me when you chose to read rather than go exploring with me."

"Yes, I guess I've often preferred the world of books over the world of people. It's starting to get dark, so we should probably get back to the motel and make an early start. We can probably finish reading Mother's diary before we get to the Horseshoe Bay ferry, which is about a six- or seven-hour drive from the lake."

June 19, 1942

> *Two great things happened today. My diary, which has been lost since January, reappeared. It was hidden among Laura's books. She said that she wanted to surprise me, so she printed all the words she knew and drew pictures on the blank pages. It was a relief to know that nobody else had read about my personal thoughts and feelings. Yesterday Mrs. Schmidt told me that Michael is coming from Alberta in two weeks and will stay for*

the summer. With Alfred away they need more help around the farm. Dad and Laura will also be happy to see him back.

July 14, 1942

Michael, Laura, Mom and Dad and I spend most Sundays together. We meet him at Mass and then he comes back to our house for the day. Mom is back from Regina and Dad is back at the store, so I don't feel guilty about taking a day off to relax. Michael is a welcome guest at our table. In fact, he seems more like family than company. Again, Laura adores him, and he is so patient with her, never tiring of her constant requests for books, piggyback rides and walks. He is not as handsome as Alfred, but much gentler and more considerate. I wish I had known Michael before I met Alfred. With Alfred being gone so long I feel like a widow, but not a grieving one.

August 16, 1942

Today we went to the annual church picnic. We invited Mrs. Schmidt, but her husband made such a fuss that she decided to stay home. Michael said, "I really feel sorry for her. There is no joy, laughter or love in that house. When Mr. Schmidt thinks that I'm not around he berates and shouts at her, and

I've seen bruises on her arms and legs, which she usually tries to cover up. I can't always prevent his abuse, but being there, talking and taking on some of the chores gives her a little relief."

Despite rationing, the tables were piled high with yummy food. There were games for everyone, young and old—horseshoes, tug of wars, baseball, spoon and egg and three-legged races. Father Jean Luc was in his glory. He has often said that his greatest happiness comes from seeing other people happy. People with cameras wandered around taking pictures, and many of the elderly and veterans were content to watch and visit with their friends. An unsettling presence was the attendance of three local boys who had been wounded and sent home. One was missing a leg and the other two were badly scarred.

August 31, 1942

Next week Michael returns to Calgary and I can't bear the thought of spending the next year without him around. After Sunday Mass, we were all going to go to the farm to fill the water jugs and weed the garden It's been a dry year and the well water is more alkaline than usual. Laura woke up with a cold and Dad wasn't feeling well, so Mom said to go without them. At the farm, we didn't intend for it to happen, but somehow we ended up embracing and kissing. Michael said, "I love you, Elizabeth, and next summer when I come back we'll plan a future together." I told him that I loved him too and wanted nothing more than to spend the rest of my life with him.

"Laura, this isn't just another Michael. I think it's possible that he was Mother's Michael, and I might be his son."

"You could be right, Matt. Keep reading and maybe we will find the truth."

CHAPTER 19

"That's odd, Laura. The next diary entry is dated almost a year later than the last one, and it looks like some pages have been torn out."

July 27, 1943

It's been almost a year since I last wrote. After Michael left I didn't have the heart for much of anything. I tried to keep up with my diary but rereading what I wrote seemed like a lot of self-pitying drivel, so I put the diary aside, intending to get back to it when I was in a better mood. This last year has been one of ups and downs, but mainly downs. The war drags on with no end in sight. Dad is not doing well, so I am at the store almost every day, and with no Sundays to look forward to work has become my whole

> *life. My only break is the few hours I spend with Laura, who also misses Michael. I was counting the months until he comes back, but in April he wrote to say that his dad had suffered a stroke and he would probably have to spend the summer in Edmonton helping his mother look after him. I wonder when the next disaster will strike.*

"Poor Mother, all her dreams falling apart and not much to look forward to. It's not surprising that she was depressed. You know, Matt, when I was younger I naively assumed that people's misfortunes and the world's problems could be easily explained and solved. People got sick because they lived unhealthy lifestyles, children misbehaved or went astray because they had poor parenting, businesses went under because they practiced slipshod management. When we were young, wasn't it wonderful to have all the answers? Then life happens, and gradually you find yourself having more questions than answers and many of your previous assumptions are shattered. Now I often find myself asking why.

"Why are some babies born healthy while others are born sickly or deformed? Why is a farmer's crop destroyed by a hailstorm while his neighbour's farm remains untouched? Why do some people live in abject poverty while others wallow in luxury? Why do young people die of cancer, heart attacks or wars that are not of their making, while some people live to healthy old ages? Why didn't God rescue his chosen people from the horrors of the concentration camps?"

"I certainly don't have any answers, Laura. I read somewhere that animals don't question the destructive forces that befall them, but with mute assent they surrender to their fate. However, humans are constantly rebelling against their fate and often turn to religion, philosophy, science, legends or myths for answers, which often don't suffice. Many of us ask the perennial questions: where did we come from, why are we here, and what will happen to us after we die? Have you ever asked yourself any of those questions?"

"Yes, for sure. With all life's ups and downs and so much tragedy in the world, it's only human to wonder if there is any reason or purpose to it all. I think if you asked Father Jean Luc those questions, he would say, 'Our purpose here on earth is to learn how to respect and love all of God's creation.'"

August 20, 1943

The town waits in suspense as news of the raid on Dieppe seeps through. For the first time since the war began, the Canadian infantry was sent into battle. Alfred will be happy. All we have heard from him since he was sent overseas are complaints about the poor food, accommodation and boredom. Most of the men from our area are in the army.

August 24, 1943

The Dieppe raid was a disaster and the Second Canadian Division was thoroughly routed. Three thousand men were killed, and an equal number were injured or taken captive. Some of the local families have already received sad news from the war office. Mrs. Schmidt is beside herself worrying about Alfred.

September 10, 1943

We have just heard that Alfred was badly wounded in the Dieppe raid, and that once he is discharged from hospital in England, he will be coming home. I wonder if this will affect the plans that I have made for my future, which doesn't include Alfred.

October 17, 1943

I saw Mrs. Schmidt at Mass today and she is overjoyed that her son is alive. She has ordered a hospital bed from the Red Cross and is fixing up a room for Laura and me. She said, "Between the two of us, we should be able to care for him and he will be happy to have his wife and daughter close by." I shall see what Alfred thinks about that! He won't be happy to be under his father's thumb again and probably regrets that he is saddled with a wife and daughter. I can't see Laura and me living in that cheerless house, but we will stay while he needs care.

I told Laura that her father was coming home and she said, "Michael coming." I worry about leaving Dad alone in the store, but I can probably get away for a few hours most days, and if the situation proves impossible, Mom said that I am always welcome at home.

November 21, 1943

Three days ago, the Schmidts picked up Alfred from the hospital in Regina. He is in worse shape than we had expected. His head is swathed in bandages and his leg is in a cast from foot to hip. I feel sorry for him but not sorry enough that I can see a future for us. Dad said that I can use their car for as long as needed, so thank God we won't be stuck at the farm with no means of escape. As well, we will have to come to town for baths and laundry, as the Schmidts have no indoor plumbing. The outhouse will be more than enough of a challenge, especially in winter.

December 1, 1943

Alfred has been home for three weeks and I don't think he's spoken more than ten words to me. It's as if I and Laura aren't there. His mother waits on him hand and foot, but except for bringing him cigarettes and booze his dad makes himself scarce. I try to help with the cooking, cleaning, hauling water and other chores. Other than Laura's prattle, mealtimes are largely silent. Every three days I drive into town to help Dad and I buy groceries, using my ration coupons to supplement the meagre food supply at the farm. Laura doesn't laugh or smile as much, and if I don't take her with me to town she throws a fit.

December 22, 1943

Yesterday Dr. Armstrong removed Alfred's bandages, and if all goes well his cast can come off in a few more weeks. His face, neck, chest and hands are badly scarred, and he will probably need his crutches for many months. I saw Alfred looking at himself in the mirror and then he shut himself in his room for the rest of the day. His good looks were so much of his self-image, he probably doesn't know who he is anymore.

December 27, 1943

On Christmas Eve, Mom, Dad, Laura and I went to Midnight Mass and then onto Leblanc's Réveillon celebration. Mrs. Schmidt wouldn't come, as Alfred refuses to leave the house and she didn't want to leave him alone with his dad. Nobody said anything about a Christmas tree, presents or Santa, so after the party Laura and I went home with Mom and Dad. Laura was entranced with the candles on the tree and as usual she was showered with gifts. I stayed for Christmas dinner, and when I came back to the farm on Boxing Day there was no sign of any celebration. Alfred was silent and surly, even when Laura showed him her Christmas toys. After the men had gone to bed I gave Mrs. Schmidt an Afghan, which Mom had crocheted for her, and a set of coffee mugs. She was so pleased but felt bad that she didn't have gifts for Laura and me. I don't think there has ever been much gift-giving in this dreary home.

"Now, I can feel sorry and some empathy for Alfred. Growing up in such a dreary, unloving home where nothing was celebrated and with an alcoholic father who beat his mother, and probably him, it's not surprising that Alfred was damaged. It would probably take a miracle for him to ever recover from such a miserable childhood."

CHAPTER 20

January 21, 1944

I think I'm living in a bad dream. Over the last three weeks there has been one storm after another, and the temperature has dropped down to minus 41 degrees. The roads are blocked, and my car is buried under three feet of snow. Even with the living room fireplace and the kitchen stove going full blast, the house is chilly, and the windows are covered with thick frost. All day Alfred sits on the couch drinking and smoking, and the house reeks of tobacco. Mr. Schmidt spends his days in the barn with the animals. Twice a day I put on layers of clothing, go outside, clear the snow off my car and shovel the path to the outhouse. With these temperatures my car won't start, but as soon as it warms up and the snowplows come through I'll drive to town, spend a few days at home and help Dad at the store.

"Do you remember the storms at the lighthouse, Laura?"

"Yes. I loved watching the winds churn up towering waves and bend the trees as if they were gyrating in a frenetic mating dance. The house was warm and cozy, and I could curl up in a chair beside the stove and read to my heart's content. On those wild days Mom always made cocoa and cinnamon buns."

"It was during and after the storms that beachcombing was at its best. One day I came across the wreckage of a ship and wondered whether anyone had survived. That day or earlier, we had not received any distress calls. Later we heard that an un-crewed ferry ship in Tofino had slipped its moorings, broken up on the rocks and drifted out to sea."

February 9, 1944

It is only fifteen below today and I can hear the snowplows. I have dug out and started the car, so once the road is cleared I will head to town. Over the last month, to keep myself sane I have been teaching Laura her numbers and letters. She learns quickly and can count to fifty, sing the alphabet and read quite a few words. She has gone through her books dozens of times, so when we are in town I must pick up a new supply.

February 28, 1944

Yesterday I took Alfred to town to see the doctor. He kept his scarf wrapped around his head and avoided making eye contact with anyone. No longer is he the dashing Alfred that they once knew, and even though some of his friends are more wounded and disabled than he is, he avoids them. Dr. Armstrong said his leg has healed well, and in time his scars will fade.

So far he shows no interest in me or sex and has not suggested that I move into his room. I am thankful for small mercies. Now that he is almost better I can begin to think about my future. There is no way that I can continue living in this house for much longer.

March 23, 1944

Today is the spring equinox and the days are getting longer. Alfred shows no signs of wanting to help around the house or farm or getting on with his life. He is always complaining about how weak and tired he is. Michael's father died shortly before Christmas, so he will be coming back to the farm as soon as he gets his mother settled. YAY!

April 12, 1944

Last night at the dinner table Alfred and his father got into a shouting match. Mr. Schmidt said that Alfred was well enough to do some chores but was just playing on his injuries. Alfred threw his plate at him and then upset the table. When Mrs. Schmidt tried to intervene, Alfred shouted, "Shut up, bitch," and Mr. Schmidt punched Alfred. Laura started to cry so I picked her up and drove home. When I returned to the farm two days later, everyone was subdued. Alfred didn't seem to care that I was leaving. His only comment was, "I don't understand how you could be so stupid as to get yourself pregnant."

May 1, 1944

After Mass I drove to the homestead, intending to do the spring cleanup. Mom and Dad were going to Regina to see her sister and took Laura with them. Soon after I started raking Michael showed up with lunch. A hello kiss and hug soon turned into much more and I am still trembling. I never dreamed that lovemaking could be so wonderful. It was the opposite of what I had experienced with Alfred. Michael is so considerate, so gentle so passionate, and he aroused feelings in me that I never suspected were there. How will I ever hide this new awakened me from my family and friends?

May 15, 1944

We're at the homestead again, this time with Laura in tow. She loves Michael and Michael loves her. After Laura went down for her nap we made love again and it was as exhilarating as the first time. Michael has accepted a teaching job in New Brunswick and wants Laura and me to go with him in September. I don't know how Alfred will react if I ask him for a divorce. He doesn't love me, but he thinks he owns me and will be very jealous if he finds out about Michael. I also don't know if I can leave Mom and Dad.

June 28, 1944

I think I'm pregnant—six weeks with no period and my breasts are tender. Thankfully I don't have morning sickness, as that would be hard to hide. When I see Michael on Sunday I'll tell him that I'm pregnant and will leave with him in September for New Brunswick.

July 18, 1944

Laura and I have been at the homestead for three days cleaning the house and weeding the garden which Mom planted over a month ago. It's the least I can do for Mom and Dad after all they have done for me. They will be heartbroken to see us go, but maybe one day we can be together again. I won't tell them anything until just before we leave.

A storm is brewing. The wind is howling, the sky is black, and I hear thunder in the distance. When Michael comes I must tell him to put his car in the barn. Prairie storms can bring hailstones, which sometimes are big enough to flatten grain fields, break windows and dent trucks and cars. Right now I'm going to put my diary in a cookie tin and hide it in the root cellar. That way there will be no chance of anyone reading it before we leave.

"And that, Laura is the last entry in Mom's diary. I'm happy that Father Jean Luc was able to fill in the blanks. Knowing what we do about Alfred's temper and his deathbed confession, we can probably assume that when he found Mom and Michael together he went crazy, killed Michael and lit the house on fire. Somehow Mom escaped and made her way to the lighthouse."

"I wish that I had known this story years ago. I always assumed—wrongly as it turns out—that Mother didn't love me, but I think that, because I resembled Alfred, whenever she looked at me she was probably filled with guilt and remorse."

Assumption

"Yes, Laura, you could be right. If I resembled my father, when she looked at me she saw Michael and the life and love that could have been hers."

"All these years I've believed that if Mother didn't love me, I must be unlovable. What happened to me at university confirmed that belief and I decided I would never put myself in a position to be hurt again."

"Now maybe we can finally move on and choose the lives we want to live."

EPILOGUE

"I'm so glad that you were able to come, Laura. I wish that we had been able to spend more time together after we took Mom's ashes to the lighthouse."

"I've been looking forward to seeing you since we parted a year ago."

"Me too. I have so much to tell you."

"Well, just by looking around I can tell it's been a busy year for you."

"Yeah, it sure has. When you said you would sell the Schmidt farm and insisted that I take the homestead, I had my doubts. In October I revisited the property and was smitten by the landscape, with its vast open skies and seas of windswept rolling grass. I was reminded of the ocean's expansive swell around the lighthouse, and I thought that maybe, after all my years of being a vagabond, it might be time to settle down. I've never farmed, but over the years I've usually succeeded at whatever I've set my mind and hand to. Over the winter

I rented a room in town, worked at the hardware store and drew up plans for a house and the land. Now the house is built and soon I will be clearing the property. At least over half of it is rented out, which provides me with some income, and I'm thinking that next spring I'll plant a garden and grow organic vegetables and fruit."

"How are you fixed for money, Matt?"

"I'm OK. You have been very generous. With a share of some of the proceeds from the sale of the Schmidt farm, and my savings, I was able to build and furnish the house, and I'll continue working at the hardware store until the garden provides a reliable income. I've been doing research and it seems that there's a growing demand for organic produce. Now, enough about me. How are things with you?"

"I'm getting closer to finding out about my daughter. Also, I've met a man I like very much. He's a librarian, a widower, and has two grownup children, so I'll see where that goes. Meanwhile, we share lots of interests and he is a good companion. A lot of my questions and doubts about Mother and our history have been answered, and I feel more at peace with myself. I'm glad that you have planted lilac bushes around your house. Whenever I inhale their scent, I'm reminded of something I can't put my finger on, but which makes me feel happy."

"I'm glad for you, and I also feel more at peace. Sometimes I'm lonely, but now that I'm settled I hope to meet some neighbours and maybe even a compatible women friend. Last week I saw a grey-haired man cleaning up around Mom's grave site, but before I could reach him he drove away."

"Was that the same man who is limping down the driveway now?"

"Yeah, that looks like him. I wonder what he wants. You don't suppose it's—hurry, open the door, Laura."

"Good morning. I'm Michael Miller. I used to know the people who owned this property."

"Yes, I know. You are Alfred Schmidt's cousin from Alberta. I'm Laura. We knew each other about thirty-five years ago."

"And I'm Matthew. Elizabeth was our mother."

"No, no, that can't be! Elizabeth and Laura died in a horrific fire thirty-five years ago."

"That's what everyone assumed, and until just a few minutes ago we also assumed that you had died in the same fire"

"How can this be possible? And where is Elizabeth now?"

"Sadly, she died of cancer last year, as did my father, Alfred. But come in and sit down. We know that this is devastating news, but we will tell you about all that has happened to us in the last thirty-five years. Matthew, would you put the coffee on? Michael, you must have as many questions as we have for you."

"Elizabeth was pregnant with my child. Do you know what happened to it?"

"Yes, that child is Matthew. He was born seven months after the fire."

"Oh, merciful God! Are you really my son?"

"Yes I am, but until we read Mom's diary last year, I didn't know. Mother told us that our father had died in the war."

As Michael and Matthew embraced, their tears flowed until after a time the truth became their reality. Michael kept repeating, "My son, my son," and a glow lit up Mathew's face.

"Michael, last year we found Mother's diary, which she had hidden in the root cellar, so we knew about your relationship. What we don't know is how Mother, Laura and you escaped from the fire."

"All I remember is Alfred exploding with anger when he found Elizabeth and me together. While he bolted out to the truck, Elizabeth ran into the bedroom to get you Laura, and when he came back with his gun he shot me twice. I must have passed out. When I came to the house was ablaze, and I just managed to crawl out to the grass and call for Elizabeth. I passed out again, and when I woke it was dark and stormy, and the barn and house were gutted by the fire. In time I made it out to the road, where a passing truck driver picked me up and took me to the hospital in Regina. I assumed that Elizabeth and Laura died in the fire, but she must have rescued the car from the barn before it burned to the ground. She would have been terrified of Alfred returning and killing her and Laura. Maybe she decided to drive to the lighthouse, where she knew they would be safe."

"That's it! That's why when we were driving back to B.C. last summer I felt that I had seen the landscape before. You kept telling me, Matt, that I had never been there before, but I knew I had."

"While I was in hospital I saw a newspaper clipping about the fire, and Elizabeth's and Laura's obituaries, which confirmed what I had already assumed. When the hospital questioned me about my burns and wounds I was too mute with grief to even make up a credible story. I thought that if Albert found out that I was still alive he might try to kill me again, so I couldn't even go back to my parents' home. As soon as I was sufficiently healed I escaped to New Brunswick, where there was a job waiting for me. Every year during my summer holiday I would drive out west, stopping at the homestead for a few hours to tend the gravesite. It's been a lonely life. I never married. My heart and mind were too filled with guilt and the memory of Elizabeth to let anyone replace her. Last year when I was here, I saw Alfred's obituary in the newspaper and an ad for his farm. Lord knows why, but I bought it, retired and moved here in July."

"Sadly, Michael, all of us have been the victims of our assumptions. Now that we know the truths about the past, maybe we can tell ourselves a new story and move on. If it's okay with you, Matt, I'll lend Michael Mother's diary, and when he has read it we will talk again."

"Good idea. We've had a year to absorb, believe and accept the information that we learned from Father Jean Luc and Mother's diaries. It will take some time for Michael to do likewise. Deep down I realize that what I have been missing and craving for many years is a sense of identity and belonging. Now I feel that a door has been opened to a place I know as home, a place where I belong to a family. When we were at the lighthouse and I went off exploring, Uncle Alex would always say to me as I went out the door, 'Haste ye home, laddie,' and so I repeat his words, 'Haste ye home, laddie.' Or should I say Dad?"

"My sentiments exactly, Matthew. I couldn't have expressed them any better."

www.ingramcontent.com/pod-product-compliance
Lightning Source LLC
LaVergne TN
LVHW041637060526
838200LV00040B/1610